Liz looked at Laura intently. "You know, I think Bradley Johnson is interested in you."

Laura ran her hand through her short, dark curls. "Oh, Liz, you've got the wrong Pearl. The guys always fall for Jacqui, not me."

Liz shook her head. "Laura, Brad isn't interested in Jacqui." She paused for a moment, and then continued. "Look, I know that you went through an awful time with Michael. I mean, we all felt terrible for you. But maybe—" Liz almost added that it was time for Laura to let herself look at another boy, but seeing the flicker of pain in Laura's eyes, she stopped herself before the words came out. Liz bit her lip. "Well, uh," she said, "Don't pay any attention to me. It doesn't really matter anyway."

FAWCETT GIRLS ONLY BOOKS

SORORITY GIRLS

Sorority Girls

STARTING OVER

Anne Hunter Lowell

FAWCETT GIRLS ONLY • NEW YORK

A Fawcett Girls Only Book
Published by Ballantine Books
Copyright © 1986 by Cloverdale Press, Inc. and Terri Fields

Library of Congress Catalog Card Number: 85-91215

ISBN 0-449-13001-0

Manufactured in the United States of America

First Edition: April 1986

To Lori Michelle Fields, with pride in the way she thinks for herself.

Chapter 1

*E*veryone stopped talking when Susie Madden tapped her pearl-handled gavel on the table in the front of the room. "I hereby call tonight's meeting to order," she said. The members of the most exclusive sorority in Taft High School rose to their feet. In unison, they repeated the secret sorority pledge that began each meeting. "We promise to uphold the things that Pearl stands for: P for pride, E for elegance, A for as one, R for respect, and L for loyalty. To Pearl we pledge them all."

When the ritual was finished, the girls sank back into their seats in the Maddens' family room, and the meeting began. Although everyone had been laughing and gossiping since they'd arrived, the mood now became serious. No one took sorority meetings lightly. After all, being selected as a member of Pearl meant you were the epitome of what every girl wished she could be. And every member of the sorority knew she had to work hard to keep her image just that way. If that meant following the traditions and rituals of the sorority and giving Pearl meetings respect, it was a small price to pay.

Susie pushed a strand of her wavy blond hair away from her face. As president, it was her duty—and, she felt, an honor—to run the meetings. She did so with a firm hand. "We have a very fine pledge class this year," she announced, "and I'm sure that by the time they go active, they'll be wonderful sisters."

Elfin Laura Clark sat at the back of the room and smiled at Susie. It couldn't be easy for her to talk about the new pledge class when her own sister had been left out, but Susie was handling the matter with dignified calm. Laura was proud of Susie and a little sad. Just the other night, she'd tried to explain to her friend, Debbie Madura, that the one thing that bothered her about Pearl was how much it hurt some girls when they didn't get in. They wanted to be members so badly and then weren't asked to pledge.

"Trust me," Debbie reassured her. "If we didn't ask them to pledge, it's because they wouldn't fit in. And if they wouldn't fit in, they wouldn't be happy here even if we had asked them to pledge."

Laura wasn't quite sure she agreed with Debbie, but on the other hand, the Pearls had always been wonderful friends to her. And it pleased her that the sorority had worked so many long hours at the hospital, too.

Realizing she'd let her attention wander from the business at hand to other thoughts, Laura turned and listened once again to what Susie was saying. "The most important thing we have to do tonight is elect a pledge trainer; she will be in charge of getting the pledges ready to become active Pearls. I know I don't have to tell you how important that job is." Susie paused and debated whether to say more. It was really important that the pledge trainer be organized, responsible, and dedicated to her job. But Susie didn't want to lecture, so she simply added, "I'm opening the floor for nominations."

The Pearls' phone conversations over the past few nights had been filled with speculations, because they already knew that the election would be held that night. Many of them had been talking for days about who would probably be nominated. It was quite an honor to be chosen pledge trainer, because it showed that your sisters in Pearl believed that you could mold and preserve the future of the sorority. Of course, the job involved a tremendous amount of work, too. And many of the girls who would have liked the honor or the title simply didn't have the time to do the job well. The pledge trainer had to attend not only all of the functions for active Pearls but all the pledge functions, as well.

Debbie Madura's hand quickly shot up in the air. "I nominate Laura Clark. She was really great

as rush chairperson." Several girls nodded in agreement, and after Laura blushingly accepted the
nomination, it looked as if she might be the only
candidate. Debbie beamed at Laura, as if to say
that she knew she'd been right to encourage her
to think about becoming pledge trainer.

Susie looked around the room, but no other
hands were raised. She almost sighed with relief.
The president and pledge trainer had to work together frequently, and Susie knew that Laura was
such a kind, thoughtful person that working with
her would be easy. However, sorority rules required that Susie asked for nominations one final
time. "This is the last call for nominations. If
there are no further nominations, Laura Clark will
be elected pledge trainer without opposition," she
said in an even voice. Susie raised her gavel and
looked out at her sorority sisters. She saw Julie
Windham catch Paula's eye. Perhaps no one besides
Susie even noticed it, but she saw Paula nod ever
so slightly. Then Julie's hand shot up in the air.

"I nominate Paula Parker," Julie said. Paula
smiled slightly and accepted the nomination. There
were some murmurs of surprise—it was obvious
that most of the girls had not considered the
possibility that Paula might want the job.

Putting aside her own disappointment at the
turn of events, Susie announced that—as they
always had to—the two girls who had been nominated would leave the room while the voting was
done. Paula and Laura rose from their seats and
headed for the door. As she left the room, Paula

was certain that no one could possibly have noticed the way she'd carefully positioned herself behind Laura so that Paula would be the one to shut the door. She closed it ever so carefully, making sure that she'd left it just enough ajar to be able to hear who was saying what about her. But Paula's cleverness was for nothing. The two girls had only been standing in the hallway for a moment when Laura said, "Gee, I don't think you shut the door all the way," and she pulled it tightly closed.

Paula's expression showed not a trace of worry. She knew Laura would never suspect that she'd purposely left it open. And hearing what everyone said didn't really matter, anyway. Paula was sure that Julie would tell her exactly what had been said, and that would be almost as good as hearing it firsthand.

On the other side of the door, Susie opened the floor for comments about the candidates. Sometimes election discussions got pretty catty, so Susie warned, "We'll have one person speak for and one person speak against both Laura and Paula. But, please, let's remember to keep the comments clear and to the point. Who'd like to begin?"

Debbie waved her hand, and so did Julie. But since they'd done the nominating in the first place, Susie passed over both of them to give some of the other girls a chance. Monica Malone stood up when Susie called on her. "Last year, Paula fell just a few votes short of being elected president of Pearl. I think that says something about how much everyone respects her. Besides, she is organized and effective, and, most important, she'd really keep the pledges on their toes. I'm sure Paula could make them see how special it is to be a Pearl."

Ellen McCormick spoke for Laura, saying, "If it hadn't been for Laura, we'd have never won that community-service award from the mayor last spring. We all know that she also pitched in and did all the little extras that made us look outstanding." Ellen and Laura had been friends for years, and Ellen loyally continued. "There's not a girl here who doesn't know how sweet and sensitive Laura is. She always has time for everyone else's problems, and I know that all the pledges would just love her."

"I think Laura's sensitivity could be a problem," Jacqui Hodgkins broke in. "I like Laura, but sometimes she's too nice. As her sorority sister, I love how concerned she is for everyone else's feelings, but I think we need a stronger personality to be pledge trainer. After all, those new pledges need to become a lot more unified before they're ready to be actives."

"Okay," Susie said, "I guess that counts as a con for Laura, so we'll take one con for Paula, and then we'll vote."

Liz raised her hand. "I think that sometimes Paula gets kind of carried away with power." She wanted to say more, but she held back. Liz knew that whatever she said would get back to Paula in spite of the sorority rules against it. She'd watched what Paula had done to Susie and her sister during rush, and she knew that Paula was not an enemy to be taken lightly.

To the two girls waiting outside the door, time seemed to be moving very slowly. Laura smiled at Paula, and there was a soft warmth in her ebony eyes. "I think this is probably the worst part of being nominated for something. I mean, it's not so bad once you know the results, but the waiting is terrible." Sighing deeply, she added, "Still, I guess there are some benefits to being out here instead of in there. I always feel bad that I have to vote for one sister and against another. But at least out here I don't have to deal with that whole problem."

Paula fidgeted with the big leather belt that was loosely buckled around her overshirt. "Yeah, it does do that," she said. And she thought for the millionth time that Laura could find something good to say about almost anything. She chuckled to herself as she wondered what Laura would think of her reason for running for pledge trainer. At first, Paula hadn't even given any thought to the job, but the previous night it had dawned on her that it might be the one sure way to eventually beat Susie Madden in a rematch in the race for the presidency of Pearl.

Nervousness kept Laura talking. "I hadn't even thought about being pledge trainer until the other day, but I have to say that since then it's been on my mind a lot. The thing I think I'd like the best is getting to work with the new girls—with all their enthusiasm. They're all so thrilled to be part of Pearl that it makes me feel excited, too."

"Uh-huh." Paula nodded her head absently, deep in her own thoughts. "Well, I think being pledge trainer could be a lot of fun for a number of reasons," she said. Then she turned to Laura and smiled. "We all know this group of pledges certainly needs to learn a lot. And whichever one of us wins this election will have a big job."

Both girls jumped as the door opened and they were invited back into the room. Susie waited as both Paula and Laura took their seats. She wasn't exactly pleased with the results of the election, but she had to announce them. Still, no one would ever know how disappointed she was. Her face showed no emotion, just a bland smile. "Our new pledge trainer is Paula Parker," she said. "Congratulations, Paula."

Paula glowed. "Thanks, everyone. I promise you I'll make sure the pledge class will be really sharp. You have my word on that."

Susie thought absently, I'll bet you will. There was little doubt in Susie's mind that Paula planned a rematch for the presidency in January. And as pledge trainer, she'd be working very closely with all the new Pearls. It would only be natural for them to want her for president. If only Laura had won! Well, I can't worry about that right now, Susie told herself firmly. She moved on to the next order of business.

"Sorry," Debbie whispered to Laura, "I still think you'd have been much better."

Laura winked back and whispered, "Thanks for nominating me." Laura was glad to have a friend like Debbie, and she told herself that even though she'd really have liked being elected pledge trainer, it wouldn't be the end of the world that she hadn't been. The Pearls were her friends, and she knew that they hadn't voted for Paula instead of her to be mean or malicious. Besides, it would give her more time to concentrate on the hospital community-service project, and that was really her first love, anyway.

The meeting continued with a treasurer's report and an evaluation of the last party they'd had with the Taft Club boys. By far the best-looking, most desirable boys at school, the boys of the Taft Club fraternity frequently had social functions with Pearl. The discussion about their last party together was lively. Finally, Julie Windham, who was recording the minutes of the meeting, threw up her hands. "I can't get all this down. Can't I just say that everyone had a great time and recommend that we plan another social activity with the Taft Club soon?"

"I'd second that," said Monica. There was a unanimous show of hands in favor of the idea.

"The next thing on the agenda is the hospital community-service project," Susie announced. "Laura?"

Opening her notebook, Laura rose to speak. "We're a little short on hours this month. I know that everyone has a lot to do, but the hospital really depends on our help. After the meeting tonight, it would really be great if all of you could sign up for at least a couple of hours next week."

"We should have Paula get the pledges started volunteering right away, don't you think?" asked Jacqui. "That would definitely increase our community-service hours."

There were a few snickers around the room. It was well known that Jacqui, despite her good intentions, always seemed to find excuses for not going over to the hospital. But on the whole, the girls decided that involving the pledges immediately was an excellent idea.

Working at the hospital wasn't exactly at the top of Paula's list of things to have the pledges do right away, but she supposed there'd be time for her projects, too. "No problem," Paula said to the group. "I'll bring volunteer work up at their first pledge meeting. In fact, Laura, would you like to come and explain to the pledges what we do at the hospital? I'm sure your enthusiasm would really get them interested."

"Do you really think so?" Paula nodded. "Then I'd be happy to. I mean, if you don't think it would intrude," Laura said.

"Not at all," Paula assured her.

The meeting ended, and the girls flocked toward the table at the back of the room for refreshments. Silver trays were laden with miniature French pastries, and silver pitchers contained milk, tea, coffee, and punch. Carla, the Maddens' maid, was standing nearby to make sure that everyone got served. To some, the scene might have seemed a little formal. After all, silver trays were not really necessary when serving refreshments to high school girls. But when Mrs. Madden had been a Pearl, her mother had served her friends that way. And she was quite certain that someday, when Susie had a daughter in Pearl, they would still be doing things exactly the same way.

Finishing a chocolate croissant, Liz spotted Laura. "Hey, Laura, I'm sorry about the election tonight."

"Oh, thanks, Liz, but it's okay. You can't win every time," Laura said without a trace of bitterness. "Besides, did you see the way Paula tried to make me feel better by inviting me to the pledge meeting to explain the hospital program?"

Liz just smiled. Laura always saw the best in everyone, and if Liz had told her that Paula had probably only wanted to get out of having to do the explanations and scheduling herself, Laura would never have believed it. Liz changed the subject. "You know, I think Bradley Johnson is interested in you."

Laura ran a hand through her short, dark curls. "Oh, Liz, you've got the wrong Pearl. The guys always fall for Jacqui, not me."

Liz looked at her. "Laura, Brad isn't interested in Jacqui." She paused for a moment and then continued. "Look, I know that you went through an awful time with Michael. I mean we all felt terrible for you. But maybe—" Liz had almost added that maybe it was time for Laura to let herself look at another boy, but seeing the flicker of pain in Laura's eyes, she stopped herself before the words came out. Liz bit her lip. "Well, uh," she said, "don't pay any attention to me. It doesn't really matter, anyway."

Chapter 2

◌━◌━◌

*L*aura didn't think much about Liz's comment about Brad. Still, she had to admit that she, like the rest of the girls at Taft High, had definitely noticed him. His six-foot frame, wavy blond hair, and deep blue eyes fringed by thick, dark lashes had made him the center of attention from the moment he'd transferred to Taft from someplace in Colorado. Within a few weeks, it was obvious that he had quite a sense of humor. And his natural ability at sports had the coaches falling all over themselves to have him on their team. The boys of the prestigious Taft Club had decided right away that they definitely wanted him as a member. But to their complete surprise, Brad hadn't jumped at the chance to join the fraternity. He'd been told at basketball practice that the guys in Taft were willing to take him in as a pledge even though he wasn't a freshman, and Brad had responded by saying, "Thanks. You're a great group of guys, and being asked to join is a real honor. But I just don't think I'd really like going through a whole pledge semester with guys who are so much younger than me. I hope we can all still hang out sometimes, though." Brad had then proceeded to make six perfect baskets.

Jacqui had heard all this from her boyfriend, Danny Martin, who had sworn her to secrecy. He wasn't supposed to tell her any Taft Club business, but it had just come out somehow. Of course, Jacqui had innocently passed it on to Susie—just in case the same situation should arise in Pearl. Susie had then mentioned it to Liz, and pretty soon Brad's position had become common knowledge among the Pearl sisters.

Jacqui couldn't find out anything more about Brad from Danny. He wouldn't tell her what had happened from there. But Brad became a Taft pledge, and then, after only three weeks, he was made an active.

"I'm glad," Jacqui had confided to Ellie. "He's just too cute not to be at the Taft Club parties!" Jacqui had also noticed that he'd never really dated just one girl since he'd transferred to Taft. Finally, she'd decided that he must still have a girl friend in Colorado. She'd planned on trying to get to know him—going out with Danny hadn't changed her that much—but their only class together was chemistry. Jacqui knew she'd be lucky to survive even if she paid attention to every word Miss McVinnis said. None of that chemical stuff made any sense to her, and Miss McVinnis was so strict that Jacqui, who usually enjoyed center stage, had tried to make herself invisible.

Even Paula, who usually manipulated teachers into seeing things her way, hadn't been able to budge Miss McVinnis. If Laura hadn't been incredibly patient and reexplained everything to her sorority sisters, Paula and Jacqui were sure they'd already be failing. Everyone said that it was the toughest class at Taft. In fact, most of the kids weren't even sure that Miss McVinnis was human; it had been rumored that she was nothing more than one of her own chemical concoctions.

"She's so old-maidish," Jacqui had said one day after class. Glacing down at her favorite boots— they were made of soft red suede—Jacqui added, "I mean, does she have to be so absolutely dowdy? Those shoes—the black lace-up ones she wears. They're just too much." Paula had gotten into the act by doing a perfect imitation of Miss McVinnis teaching; she'd even mimicked the woman's high-pitched, angry whine to a tee. Everyone had laughed, and while Laura had to admit it was funny, she really didn't think Miss McVinnis was so bad. She really knew a lot about chemistry, even if she did talk and dress funny. Sometimes Laura wondered whether Miss McVinnis had started out that strict or had just gotten tougher over the years because the kids had always given her such a hard time.

*   *   *

That day, Laura walked into chemistry class and sat down at her desk. She noticed that Miss McVinnis was wearing the ugly black shoes that Jacqui had made fun of. And her granny glasses were tilted on her nose. As the final bell rang, she stared at the class and waited for silence. Then she warned, "I think you'll all want to listen very carefully to what I'm going to say." There were apprehensive looks around the room. Everyone wondered what terrible torture she'd planned. Miss McVinnis continued. "I've planned a special experiment for today. You will use the chemical dissection process we learned to identify an unknown liquid. You and your lab partner will turn the results in to me at the end of the hour. If you know what you are doing and you do it quickly, that should be enough time." There was a collective groan from the students and scattered voiced complaints. Jacqui Hodgkins thought to herself that if she spilled so much as a drop of that stuff on the white angora sweater she was wearing, she'd just die. She hated chemistry. Nothing ever came out the way it was supposed to. During one experiment, she'd even gotten some solution on her fingers accidentally. It had turned them yellow for a week.

Miss McVinnis tapped a ruler on the desk to get the class to quiet down again. "You're wasting valuable time. Are there any questions?"

Brad Johnson raised his hand, and the teacher glared at him. "What is it, Bradley?" she asked in an impatient tone.

"Miss McVinnis, since my lab partner is absent today and so is Laura Clark's, could we work together?"

Miss McVinnis nodded wearily. "I suppose so. It will mean one less lab to clean." She then told the students to report to their lab stations. Laura watched Brad stride purposely toward hers, and all at once Liz's words came back in a rush. "I think Brad Johnson is interested in you," she'd said. Laura fought a rising blush and told herself that she was being silly. Everyone knows that it's much easier to get an experiment done if you have a lab partner to help. And judging from what Miss McVinnis had said, that day's experiment was going to be particularly difficult.

"Hi," Brad said with an easy smile. "I hope you don't mind my asking to be your partner for the day." He looked boyishly uncertain, and that pleased Laura. She hated the way most of the Taft Club boys seemed to expect girls—even Pearls—to faint if they so much as smiled at them. Still, his preppy crew-neck sweater and Bass Weejun loafers left no doubt that Brad fit in with the other boys in Taft's most prestigious fraternity.

"I don't mind at all," she said. "Actually, I really appreciate it. I've got a feeling this is going to be a tough experiment."

Brad smiled again. "Oh, I think we'll do okay." Laura hoped he was right, because although she didn't go around announcing it, she planned to become a doctor someday. Good chemistry grades would be a big edge in getting into a good pre-med program. She picked up the test tube of liquid they were supposed to identify. "Well, it has no color and no odor, so we won't get any clues that way. I guess I'll start setting up beakers, okay?"

"Sounds good to me," Brad replied. "I'll get the chemicals so we can try mixing them with the unknown."

In a few minutes, both Brad and Laura were deeply absorbed in what they were doing. They tried mixing first one chemical and then another with the liquid they'd been given, noting the reactions. "I just tried potassium chromate, and there's no reaction," Laura said.

"Okay, so there's no lead in the solution," Brad said, and scribbled the latest finding in his notebook. "Pretty soon we're bound to have it narrowed down." They went back to work. A little later, Brad glanced at the digital watch on his arm. "We've only got a few minutes left. We'd better come up with some conclusions."

Miss McVinnis's voice boomed through the room. "Okay, everyone, your time is up. Stay at your lab stations and I'll collect your notes and check to make sure everything is put away."

Laura and Brad had narrowed the unknown solution to two possibilities. Just as they scribbled down their final choice, Miss McVinnis came to their station. She looked at their paper but didn't comment on the answer. "Be sure that station gets cleaned before you leave," she said, walking on to the next pair.

"I think we got it," Brad said confidently.

"Oh, I don't know," Laura replied. "We really just guessed at the very end there. And Miss McVinnis didn't exactly look thrilled at our answer."

"I'm not sure Miss McVinnis ever looks thrilled about anything," Brad said with a laugh. The bell rang, and everyone got ready to leave. "Tell you what," he said, slinging his blue backpack over one shoulder. "I'll bet you a Coke. I'll pay if we're wrong; you pay if we're right. Sorry, I've got to run. My next class is clear across campus."

After Brad left, Jacqui sauntered over to Laura. "Hmm, looks as if you've found some unexpected benefits to chemistry."

"Oh, Jacqui, don't be ridiculous." Laura picked an imaginary piece of lint off her pale blue cashmere sweater. "We just worked on a chemistry experiment, that's all."

Jacqui's blue eyes flashed. "Laura, this is me, Jacqui. I'm your friend, remember? Besides, I saw how Brad practically begged old McVinnis to let him work with you."

Laura laughed. Jacqui was always trying to make everything into a mysterious, passionate encounter. "Jacqui, his lab partner was absent, and so was mine. That's all there was to it."

"Right"—Jacqui smiled—"and Bev Arnold's lab partner was absent, and so was Angie Gaynor's." She shifted her books from one arm to the other.

"Brad seems nice enough, and he's really good-looking, too. Laura," she said in a confiding tone, "it's time. You've got to let go of the past and be willing to give romance another try. Really."

With that, Jacqui turned to leave for her next class. But she turned in the doorway and gave Laura a searching look. "Maybe I've butted in where I don't belong, Laura. But what I'm telling you is definitely for your own good." Then, with a swing of her dark curls, she walked down the corridor.

Laura tried not to smile. Jacqui had slipped into another of her roles. For a moment, she'd really seen herself as Laura's big sister, her confidante. But Laura knew that no one mood of Jacqui's lasted too long. She prided herself on being unpredictable, and Laura was fairly certain that Jacqui would have forgotten all about her big-sister role by the end of next hour. But Laura also knew that Jacqui wouldn't have bothered to say anything if she hadn't really been concerned. And she appreciated the thought.

Still, Laura walked slowly to her next class. It was not the first time that someone had tried to talk to her about dating again. Recently, both Debbie and Ellen had urged Laura to let go of the past and go out with a boy once in a while. "I can't," she'd told them. "I just can't. Besides, I don't know why it matters whether I date or not. I go to all the parties; I have a good time." If Debbie and Ellen pushed her too far, Laura always stopped them. "Listen," she'd say, "I really appreciate what you're trying to do, and I understand what you're saying. But I'll know when I'm ready again. I really will. Besides, none of the Taft boys ever ask me. And I don't want you putting anyone up to it."

Laura was sure that the Taft boys felt as uncomfortable about dating her as she did about going out with them. Even though she was always invited to every party and people were quick to make sure that she knew she was wanted, no one boy in the group ever asked her out. It was as if they had come to see her as a solo act, and for a long time that was just the way she'd wanted it. Now she didn't know what she wanted. Suddenly, Laura remembered her bet with Brad. What had he meant? Laura told herself that it was probably just something to say and he'd forget all about it by the next day. But deep down she didn't really believe that. Brad had been flirting with her. And why shouldn't he? After all, he hadn't even been at Taft High when she'd known Michael.

Laura sighed, picked up her books, and headed for French. Chemistry, she mused, had been more fun that day than it had been all year long—it hadn't even seemed like work. Brad was certainly easy to be around. And yet, she thought, I don't want to date again. Not just yet. At least I don't think I do.

Walking into French class, Laura slid into her seat, and Debbie waved from across the room. "You're late," she mouthed. Laura smiled. She supposed she could discuss with Debbie her mixed-up feelings about boys in general and Brad in particular. But she already knew what Debbie would say. Laura straightened one of the pleats in her skirt and told herself, This is just something I'm going to have to come to terms with by myself.

Chapter 3

O∞O

*A*lthough she was sure she'd have to say some-thing to Brad in chemistry the next day, Laura still didn't know exactly what. She'd just have to play it by ear, she thought nervously as she walked into the lab. But when class started, she found she didn't have to worry about it after all. Miss McVinnis handed out a pop quiz that took the whole hour, and she didn't say a thing about the results of the previous day's lab.

Laura caught herself looking at Brad a couple of times during the test. Shaking her head, she scolded herself. I'm acting like a lovesick fresh-man or something. After class, Brad started toward her, but Paula got there first. She called out to Jacqui to join them. "I just wanted to remind you both about the meeting tonight. We've just got to get the pledge duties all set. I tell you, those girls are going to need a lot of help before they're ready to be active Pearls. And I for one think we've let them go entirely too long without showing them how much they need to learn before they can become Pearls."

Jacqui grinned. "Paula, they've only been pledges for a few weeks." She paused a moment before saying, "Hey, do you guys remember our pledge prank?"

Paula laughed. "I sure do. Whose idea do you think it was, anyway?"

"Oh, that's right." Jacqui smoothed the long sweater dress she was wearing. "You did plan it, didn't you? Will you ever forget the look on Mrs. Casner's face when she saw the history classroom?" Jacqui laughed. "How'd you ever get that master key to get in the school?"

"Would you believe that I just found it lying on the sidewalk one day?" Paula's face broke into an angelic grin. With her flowing blond hair and innocent-looking blue eyes, Paula looked as if she were incapable of doing anything underhanded or mean. But those who knew her well knew better. Any girl in her pledge class could attest to the fact that it was Paula who'd come up with all the ideas for pledge pranks. And although their pledge trainer had admired Paula for her audacity, she'd vetoed most of her suggestions because she was afraid the girls wouldn't be able to pull them off. Had she known Paula better, she might have known that anything was possible.

Jacqui smiled and waved at a boy who was

passing by the doorway. Without missing a beat, she said to Paula, "The key must have just jumped up and right into your hand. Anyway, it was a great prank. Listen, girls, I've got to run or I'll get another tardy slip. But I'll definitely be ready for tonight."

Paula looked at Laura. "Me, too," Laura replied. "See you there."

Just a few hours later, the Pearls were once again seated in the Maddens' family room. The meeting was called to order. Paula looked around smugly—not a single absence. It had been worth it to contact every girl personally to make sure she'd be there. Paula wanted them all to see her train the pledges from the beginning. She wanted every one of them to see just how she'd pull the pledge class together, because Paula knew what a terrific job she was going to do. If the Pearl actives watched from step one, they'd really appreciate every single thing that she'd accomplished. Paula looked up at Susie and the gavel Madden was holding and thought to herself, Enjoy it while you've got it, Susie. It won't be yours forever.

In fact, it already gave Paula great pleasure to have Susie turn the meeting over to her and sit down while she discussed just what should be required of the pledges. "I really want everyone's input," she said, her long blond hair falling around her shoulders. What she actually meant was that she didn't mind their input as long as they allowed her to make all the final decisions. But they didn't have to know that.

Liz raised her hand. She and Susie had talked for a long time on the phone the night before, and Susie had decided that she wouldn't say anything; Paula was sure to find a way to reject any of Susie's ideas. Instead, it would be up to Liz to present Susie's ideas as well as her own. "I think we should definitely have them wear string necklaces on Thursdays, when we wear our pearls," Liz offered.

"Good idea," Paula said. It was something she'd already decided they'd do. "That will remind them that they're not Pearls yet." There was a large newsprint pad leaning against the wall, and Paula walked over to it. She wrote the days of the week at the top of the page. "That will take care of Thursday, but I really do think we should have them do something every day to prove their devotion to Pearl."

The other days remained invitingly blank, and the Pearls tossed out suggestions. Jacqui raised her hand, showing off the thick gold bracelet she wore around her wrist. "Remember when we had to have a boy walk us to and from our classes when we were pledges? Why don't we try that again?"

Monica Malone groaned. "I remember. I was the only freshman in my Spanish class, and I thought I'd die having to ask an upperclassman to walk me to my next class. I considered just never leaving Spanish."

"Oh, I don't know," Jacqui said. "I thought it was kind of fun." Jacqui had collected boys the way some girls collected stuffed animals, and she freely admitted that she had enjoyed that particular pledge activity more than any of the others. Going out with Danny had changed all that, but she still remembered those days with a smile. "Besides," she added, "how many guys at school wouldn't be flattered to be seen walking with a Pearl—even a pledge?"

After a little more discussion, the Pearls decided to make getting a boy to walk you to class the activity for Wednesdays. "Then it's settled," Paula said, her soft blue eyes gleaming. "I'll have all of the pledges keep a little notebook that they'll have to have the boy who walked them to class sign. Then I'll check the notebooks every Wednesday night at pledge meetings. But you all can help me by keeping your eyes open on Wednesdays and letting me know if you see any of our pledges in the hallway without an escort."

From then on, suggestions began to fly fast and furiously, and Paula gave careful attention to each one. No one could have guessed from her interested expression that the thing that interested her the most was just being the one who was up in front of the group and in charge. It just felt so right. Paula knew the Pearls had made a mistake not to elect her president, and by the time she was finished as pledge trainer, they'd all know it, too. Then Paula corrected herself. At least most of them will know it, she thought. Liz followed

Susie around like a little puppy dog, so it was
clear where her loyalties would be. And she probably couldn't count on Ellie, either; Ellie was fair,
but she had also known Susie for years. She
wouldn't be easy to win over.

Paula turned her attention back to the meeting.
Someone suggested, "I think on Tuesdays we
should make the pledges come to school with
curlers in their hair or cold cream on their faces."
There were some scattered giggles.

Paula rested one hand on the pocket of her
Guess jeans. "I don't know. A few of our pledges
are an embarrassment to Pearl even with their
makeup on. Especially—"

Laura interrupted Paula before she could finish. She was fairly certain what the other girl had
planned to say—Paula was going to make another jab at Molly Gold. What Paula had against
Molly, Laura wasn't sure. But she didn't see any
point in letting Paula criticize the pledge in front
of all the actives. Perhaps Molly wasn't as natu-
rally pretty as many of the Pearls, but she dressed
with a real sense of style, and she did have a
perfect complexion. "You know, Paula, I think
you've made a very good point. The Pearls do
have a certain image to maintain. And the pledges
should always strive to look their best in order to
keep up that image."

Several girls agreed. Paula, sensing the mood of
the group, said that that was exactly what she
had intended. Wearing curlers to school would
make them mindful of their appearances.

Paula prided herself on being able to figure out people pretty well, but Laura was still a bit of a mystery to her. Was she really as good and kind as she seemed? Paula doubted it. She was certain that everyone basically watched out for themselves first.

The girls then decided against making the pledges wear curlers. Instead, it was passed that they should have to carry enough gum to give any active a piece should she request it during school. And on Tuesdays the actives would be seated at the Pearl table in the cafeteria, and the pledges would have to go buy and then serve them their lunches.

"Now," said Paula, "we need something good for a Saturday, something that will teach them unity and keep them humble."

Ellen raised her hand. "How about if we bring them our laundry and they have to wash it and fold it for free? My mom would be thrilled if she didn't have to do my laundry for a week."

"Well," Paula said, smiling and trying not to let her impatience show, "that's a good idea. But I was thinking that we need to come up with something a little more—maybe a little more daring, if you know what I mean. I'd like us to plan something for the girls to make them really earn the privilege of being Pearls."

"Just what did you have in mind?" Susie asked from the back of the room. Paula couldn't keep a small frown from appearing on her face. She'd

almost forgotten about Susie; it seemed so natural to be up there running the meeting.

"Well, Susie"—Paula pushed a sleeve of her
sweater up a little—"I'm not really sure. My cousin
pledged a sorority at the University of Michigan,
and after what she told me, some of our activities
seem pretty mild."

Laura ran her hand through her short, dark
curls. She didn't like the way the meeting was
heading at all. She, too, had heard about some of
the exploits of Paula's cousin's sorority, and some
of them seemed more cruel than funny. "You
know," she said when Paula called on her, "it
seems to me that we've got quite a bit of stuff for
them to do already, and we want to leave them
enough time to do some work for our hospital
community-service project."

"Oh, they'll have time," Paula said, cutting her
off.

The discussion continued for the next few minutes, and Liz glanced over at Susie a few times
while the others were arguing. Was Susie angry
that Paula had literally taken over the meeting?
She certainly didn't look very happy, sitting in the
back of the room. Maybe Susie didn't feel that she
could do anything about it. But as her best friend,
Liz knew that she certainly could. She raised her
hand. "Paula, we've been at this for over an hour.
I move that we go with what we've got; we can
figure out some other things another time. Besides, Laura's mom made some of those Hershey's

Kiss cookies, and my stomach is growling just thinking about them."

Paula thought quickly. She hated to let the meeting end, but then she realized that if they weren't finished, Susie would have to turn the meeting over to her again another night. "Okay," she said smoothly, "I agree that we should post- pone discussion on the matter. But all of you have to promise me that you'll try to come up with a really unusual pledge duty." The matter was put to a vote, and it was decided that they'd end the meeting then.

Monica Malone raised her hand. "Before the meeting is over, I'd just like to say that I think Paula is doing a great job as pledge trainer. The pledges are lucky to have her."

Paula swung her long blond hair modestly. "Thanks for your vote of confidence. And I promise you all that I'll make this pledge class so out- standing that it will be the most unified, most imaginative class in Pearl history."

With that, Paula took her seat to a rousing round of applause, and Susie returned to the front of the room. She took over the meeting just long enough to adjourn it and ask everyone to help themselves to the refreshments.

She didn't have to ask twice. Laura's mother was well known for her baking ability. The Mad- dens' maid had arranged several dozen cookies on the silver trays, and they quickly disappeared. Susie walked over to Laura. "These are the great- est. They're worth every single calorie."

"Your mom is the greatest," Liz added, wishing that her own mother could be a little more like Mrs. Clark. Laura's mother had such a relaxed elegance about her. Liz sighed. As much as she loved her parents, sometimes it seemed to her that they viewed their daughter as their means to social acceptance in Kenilworth. In the few years they'd lived there, Liz had never seen them as excited as when she'd been invited to be a Pearl.

Liz tried to imagine what it might have been like at Laura's house when she'd gotten the invitation to pledge. Liz had the feeling that Mrs. Clark would have been happy with whatever Laura wanted to do. Of course, the Clarks had been an accepted part of Kenilworth society for a long time. Enviously, Liz thought that they'd been important people in this community almost as long as the Maddens had. Still, Mrs. Clark didn't seem nearly as proper as Mrs. Madden. And Mr. Clark certainly wasn't as intimidating as Mr. Madden. Liz had the feeling that most of the girls in Pearl would have been overjoyed to have the Clarks as parents.

Almost as if she had read Liz's mind, Susie told Laura, "Do you realize that your mom has been our room mother, our brownie leader, and our chief baker since we were all in the first grade!"

"I think she really enjoys it," Laura confided. "And it's been nice to have her get to know all my friends so well. She has been complaining lately that when we graduate and go off to college, she's going to feel as if she's losing twenty daughters instead of just one."

Laura glanced over to the table. "Gee, the cookies are all gone. I know there are more in your kitchen; I'll go get them."

"Don't worry; Carla will get them," Susie said.

"That's okay; I know just where I left them." On her way into the kitchen, Laura saw Julie and Paula huddled in conversation. They didn't notice her, and Laura didn't mean to eavesdrop, but she couldn't help overhearing bits of their conversation.

". . . the pledge prank . . . so incredible . . . the Pearls will love it," Paula said. Julie said something back, and Paula continued, "Yeah, well . . . that little Molly Gold . . . always questioning."

Laura stood in the kitchen, chewing thoughtfully on a fingernail. She had a distinct feeling of uneasiness. Now stop it, Laura, she lectured herself. First of all, you shouldn't have been listening. Second of all, Paula really didn't say anything that should give anyone a reason for concern. And third of all, you're being overly sensitive again. In spite of her firm words, Laura couldn't shake the feeling that had overtaken her. There was going to be trouble; she just knew it. But what could she do about it? She didn't have the vaguest idea what Paula was up to. Feeling helpless, Laura took the extra cookies and headed back into the other room with them.

Chapter 4

ↄ•ↄ

$\mathcal{L}$aura's uneasiness lasted through the rest of the evening, but by the next morning she had convinced herself that she was worrying about nothing. Even her best friends said she was too sensitive sometimes. And she had no real reason to believe that Paula was going to do anything but a good job with the pledges. She sat up in bed and rubbed the sleep from her eyes. Good heavens, she scolded herself, I hope I'm not reacting this way because Paula was elected pledge trainer and I wasn't.

As always, she dressed for school with great care, not to impress anyone but just because it made her feel good. She looked quickly at herself in the mirror before leaving for school. The pale lilac of her new angora sweater made her dark eyes look even more arresting. And the short curly wisps of hair that fell on her forehead emphasized the delicateness of her face. Laura put on a deep purple cloisonné bracelet and matching earrings, added a final touch of plum pink lipstick to her lips, and decided that she was ready to do. She had no illusions that she would ever have the stop-dead-in-your-tracks kind of beauty that Jacqui had. Or even Paula's angelic prettiness. In fact, she was always rather surprised when people told her she was attractive. Michael had called her his perfect princess. Laura blushed as she remembered—he was still so vivid in her mind, though it had been almost two years ago now. Glancing at the clock, Laura pushed her memories away and rushed out of the house to school.

The day passed in a relatively uneventful manner until chemistry. The bell had just rung and Miss McVinnis called for quiet when Brad began, "Uh, Miss McVinnis—"

The elderly teacher fixed him with a cold stare. "I don't remember asking for any questions."

Jeff Jones, another Taft Club boy, muttered under his breath to Paula, "When you get as old as she is, you probably don't remember very much." Paula turned and rewarded Jeff with a giggle and a wink.

"Perhaps you'd like to tell the class what you find so funny, Miss Parker." Miss McVinnis stood at the front of the room with her arms crossed.

"Nothing. I'm sorry," Paula said. But her cold

tone of voice and the fire in her eyes said that the only thing she was really sorry about was having to sit through an hour of chemistry.

"Now, Brad, what was it that was so important?" Miss McVinnis asked without acknowledging Paula's apology.

Brad flashed her his most disarming smile. "Oh, I was just wondering if you had graded our labs on the unknowns we had to analyze yet." As he asked the question, he looked not at Miss McVinnis but at Laura. And she was very aware of the faint twinkling in his deep blue eyes.

"Yes, I have," she said, "which is why we will spend the rest of this hour going over the process again. On Monday, I will hand your papers back to you, and the class will repeat the experiment— with what I hope will be more accurate results."

Laura listened carefully as the teacher went over the procedure again. It seemed to her that she and Brad had done everything just the way Miss McVinnis was explaining it. However, based on the teacher's comments, they must have done something wrong. Realizing she'd let her thoughts stray from the lecture, Laura glanced over at Paula, who seemed to be taking notes quite attentively. But looking at Paula's paper, Laura could see that the notes were only about Pearl pledge activities. Laura sighed with dismay. Paula had always hated science, but somehow she'd always charmed her way through her other science classes. Their freshman year, in biology, Paula had fainted every time they'd had to dissect something. Finally, she'd somehow convinced the teacher that since her fainting was disturbing other students, she should just be excused from lab and still get a passing grade. Everyone was a little in awe of Paula, and while they had no idea how she'd pulled it off, they knew that only Paula could have done something like that and gotten away with it. But Laura was sure that Paula had more than met her match in Miss McVinnis. She'd tried to tell that to Paula, but Paula had seemed unwilling to believe her. She was sure that even Miss McVinnis could be handled. Still, Laura shuddered to think how angry Paula's mother was going to be when Paula failed chemistry. And there was no doubt in Laura's mind that she would. Sighing, Laura hoped she could give Paula enough of the basics to at least get her a D.

She was still thinking about Paula when she left the classroom, and she didn't even notice Brad lounging against the door. "Excuse me," he said with mock severity. "Don't I owe you a Coke?" His penetratingly blue eyes remained fixed on Laura as a grin spread across his lips. "Well, I never welsh on a bet. When do I pay up?"

Laura hesitated, filled with conflicting emotions. It was no big deal, she told herself. After all, he was only asking her out for a Coke. She'd stopped off for ice cream or a hamburger with a boy many times since Michael. So why was she feeling so uncomfortable about going out with Brad? Laura couldn't answer her own question. Looking at the tall, handsome boy before her, she only knew that there was something very different from what she'd felt for those other boys stirring inside her. And she wasn't very sure that she could cope with those feelings. A sense of vulnerability ran over her; Laura hugged her books to her chest and stalled by saying, "You may not have even lost the bet. After all, Miss McVinnis hasn't even handed our papers back yet. Let's wait and see just who owes whom!"

Brad gave her a conspiratorial wink. "Okay, we'll play it your way for the time being." With that, he turned and headed for his next class.

Laura went through the rest of her classes that day feeling strangely tired. After the final bell rang, Debbie caught up with her in front of her locker. "Ellen and Liz and I are going to stop for ice cream at Le Finis—that new dessert place on Cleremont. Want to join us?"

"Well, I was thinking of putting in some extra time at the hospital this afternoon—"

Debbie interrupted, "Oh, come on, Laura. You already put in more time than everyone else combined. Get some ice cream with us. Then if you still want to go to the hospital, I'll go and put in an hour or two with you."

"That's really sweet of you, Deb. Okay, you're on!" Laura said. She slammed her locker shut, and it clanged with the finality of Friday afternoon. The two girls walked to the parking lot, swinging their book bags as they went.

"I came to school with Ellen this morning, but

I'll drive over to Le Finis with you so I can show you where it is," Debbie offered.

The two girls climbed into Laura's dark blue Camaro. "Are you sorry you didn't get red?" Debbie asked.

Laura thought for a minute. "No, not really. I think my dad was right when he said that it was a little too showy. I'm glad I got the blue, but I sure agonized over it. Remember?"

Debbie laughed. "Do I ever. We must have gone over it about fifteen times on the phone while you tried to make up your mind."

The car seemed to almost float down the wide streets, and the big trees on either side provided a haze of golden shade. "My parents were sure terrific about the whole thing. I mean, they knew that a Camaro was my dream car."

Debbie remembered the situation well. A year earlier, the Pearls had been invited to a city-council meeting by the mayor. They were to be honored as an example of what caring young people could do. Accompanied by their proud parents, the girls had gone to the meeting, which had one of the largest turnouts for a Kenilworth city-council meeting that anyone could remember.

The mayor had read a letter he'd received from the director of Kenilworth Memorial Hospital that said, in part, "In the last year, the young women in Taft High's Pearl sorority have made a tremendous difference in this hospital. They have provided a thousand hours of time and effort, and they've brought a cheerful sense of optimism to the hospital that has been an encouragement to many of our patients. As director of this hospital, I feel that the community should know of their outstanding efforts."

The mayor, who had been a Pearl herself, had given them a plaque. And since Laura had been in charge of coordinating the project, she'd been the one designated to stand in front of the council and receive it. Afterward, a newspaper photographer had asked Laura if he could get a picture of her and her parents with the mayor. The mayor was happy to oblige, but by the time she and Laura had made their way over to Mr. and Mrs. Clark, Paula was already standing with them. She'd smiled with an ingenuous naïveté. "Hi, Laura, I was just telling your mom and dad how many of those thousand hours were your personal hard work and how we'd never have been honored this way without you."

Laura blushed. "Well, I don't really think—"

The photographer cleared his throat. "Excuse me, but could we snap this picture? Then, Mayor Lipton, I'd like to get a shot of you signing the new city budget."

Paula appeared to have just noticed the photographer for the first time. "Oh, I'm so sorry. I must be in the way."

"Not at all," Mrs. Clark said firmly. "There's no reason you can't be in the picture, too. After all, the award was given to all the Pearls. In fact, my husband and I really don't belong in it at all."

And so the picture of Mayor Lipton, with Laura

on one side of her and Paula on the other, had appeared in the *Kenilworth Advance* the next day. Susie had called up Liz as soon as she'd seen it. "I know Paula did it on purpose. I know she wrangled her way in just to get the attention."

"Well, she won't get away with it," Liz said loyally. She'd then proceeded to tell practically everyone—confidentially, of course—that if anyone should have been in the picture with Laura, it should have been Susie. After all, Susie was the president of the sorority. No one really disagreed with Liz's argument, but there was nothing anyone could do about it now, and most of the girls decided it hadn't been a planned slight, anyway.

A couple of days later, Debbie had been over at Laura's house and had seen the newspaper photo taped to the refrigerator door. "You know," she'd told Mrs. Clark, "Laura never got mad at anyone who didn't put in her hours. She just put in more time herself to compensate. Really, if it hadn't been for Laura, we wouldn't have gotten that award."

Mrs. Clark had offered Debbie one of the cookies she'd just finished baking, and in spite of Laura's blush, she'd said, "We're very proud of Laura."

"Oh, Mom," Laura had protested. "You don't have to be proud. I didn't do anything so wonderful; I really enjoy working at the hospital."

Nevertheless, at breakfast a week later, Laura's parents told her to come right home after school because they had a special surprise for her. At lunch, some of the girls had tried to guess what it might be or why she was getting it, but no one even came close. That afternoon when she got home from school, her parents were both waiting for her. Laura couldn't believe that her father was there, too. His demanding job as a design engineer for General Motors left little time for taking off in the middle of the afternoon.

"Let's go, Laura," her father had said with a twinkle in his eye.

"Where are we going? What's going on? It isn't my birthday; it isn't your anniversary. Why is today so special?"

Her parents had merely smiled. "You'll see," they said, enjoying the suspense. Laura was still unsure what was going on when they pulled up in front of Kenilworth's Chevrolet dealer.

"Are you getting a new car?" she asked, feeling totally confused.

"No, honey," her father said with delight. "You are."

Laura looked first at her father and then at her mother. Her large dark eyes were questioning. "Your father and I had a long talk about all the things you always do for other people," Mrs. Clark explained. "Your work at the hospital is just one example, and, well, we wanted you to know that we're proud of the unselfish way you care about other people."

"In other words," Laura's father blurted out, "we think it's time for you to get something special just for you. So let's pick out that Camaro you've always wanted."

All of a sudden, Laura saw her mother's smiling face and her father's three-piece gray suit swimming in front of her eyes. She leaned back against the car for support. "Oh, I—I don't know what to say." They'd gone inside and picked out the model, but Laura just couldn't decide what color. Mr. and Mrs. Clark had suggested to Laura that she think about it overnight. They could come back and place the order the next day.

That night on the phone, Laura had relayed every detail to Debbie. "Can you believe it? For a minute, I thought I'd just faint on the spot. My face has been frozen in a permanent smile, and— Oh, Debbie, I have the greatest parents in the whole world."

Debbie had quickly agreed, which she would have done even if they hadn't given Laura the car. Laura's family was extremely close-knit, and her parents were always behind her and her brother, Jason, one hundred percent. Debbie and many of the other Pearls were just a little envious.

"Hey, Debbie," Laura called. "What are you daydreaming about? You haven't said a word since we got into the car. We're almost at Cleremont. Where is this place?"

Debbie sat up and looked out the window. "Sorry, I guess I was kind of lost in thought." She pointed across the street. "Turn left by the blue awning. There's parking there, and we can walk the rest of the way." Cleremont Avenue had a four-block stretch that was closed to traffic. All of the best shops in Kenilworth were located there, and the landscaped mall added to the exclusive appearance of their front windows.

The girls walked in and saw that Ellen and Liz were already seated. They waved as Debbie and Laura headed toward them. "What an adorable place!" Laura exclaimed as they sat down. "And I love these blue-and-white-striped chairs. This place is going to give the Turf a real run for its money," she added, referring to the local Taft hangout.

Ellen opened her menu. "Wait until you taste their desserts. They've got to be ten thousand calories, but they're absolutely out of this world!"

"Oh, Ellen, you don't have to worry about calories," Laura reassured her friend.

"Me, either," Liz said, sighing, "but that's because I'm built like a board."

"That's not true," Laura said. "Besides, I'd give anything to have even one-tenth of your athletic ability. The last tennis match you played—the one against that senior from Boyington—was the most exciting tennis I've ever seen anywhere."

"That *was* some match," Liz agreed. "I never thought I'd beat her." And though she didn't say so, Liz thought about how she'd felt she'd had an edge because all her sorority sisters had been there rooting for her. Sometimes she still could hardly believe that she was actually a Pearl.

The waitress walked over to the table. "Have you girls decided what you want?"

"I'll have a chocolate-filled croissant," Ellen said.

Laura's dark eyes gleamed. "Well, if I'm going to splurge, I may as well go all the way. I'll have an eclair."

When she'd finished taking their orders, the girls watched the waitress walk away. "Even their uniforms are cute. And look how thin she is. Maybe their stuff isn't all that fattening after all," Ellen said hopefully.

"Don't bet on it," said a new voice. "It's more likely that they don't let the employees taste very many samples."

"Paula!" exclaimed Laura. "When did you get here? Pull up a chair and join us."

"Thanks," said Paula, "but I'm meeting someone in a few minutes. Actually, I'm glad I ran into you, Laura. I wanted to confirm with you that you'll be at the pledge meeting on Wednesday night to tell the girls about working at the hospital."

"You're sure you want me there?"

"Absolutely." Paula's big blue eyes flashed with sincerity. "Just don't be afraid to lay it on the line and let the pledges know that you expect them to volunteer a lot of time. You don't want to be too nice, Laura. After all, they have to earn the right to wear the strand of pearls."

Before Laura could answer, Paula caught sight of a broad-shouldered, yellow-sweatered figure coming toward her. "I've got to go," she said, turning toward the boy who was approaching the table. Paula flashed him her most brilliant smile, linked her arm through his, and walked away.

"Isn't that Gil Anderson, the boy Susie dated a

couple of times when she and Mike broke up?" Ellen asked.

"Yes, but I don't think Susie ever really cared about him," defended Liz.

"He sure is cute," said Debbie. "Didn't he used to be a Taft Club guy when he was in high school?"

"I think so," said Laura. "He must be home from Northwestern for the weekend. He and Paula make a cute couple." She glanced at her watch. "Listen, I hate to break this up, but I still want to put in a couple of hours at the hospital. Anyone want to join me?"

"I will," said Debbie, her emerald eyes still focused on Paula and her date for the afternoon. "I mean, I already promised I would. Anyone else want to come?"

Ellen looked at Liz, and Liz guiltily returned the look. Both were behind on their hours of service, but it didn't seem like a very exciting way to spend a Friday afternoon. Finally, Liz said, "I guess I could put in an hour. How about you, Ellen?"

Ellen nodded her okay.

"Gee, thanks, you guys," Laura said. "I may stay a little later, so if Debbie wants to leave earlier, can she go home with you?"

"Of course," Ellen replied. The girls passed Paula, waved, and walked out the door. "I'll say this for Paula," Ellen said with a backward glance. "She sure knows how to pick guys."

Debbie and Laura climbed into the Camaro, and once again Laura felt a strange sense of unease about Paula. "Debbie," she asked after a while, "do you think Paula's taking this whole pledge-trainer thing a little too seriously?"

"Um-hum. Actually, I'm amazed at the amount of time and dedication she's putting in. I'd have never guessed she would, but to tell you the truth, I'm glad. It's nice to see her preoccupied with something besides feuding with Susie."

Laura decided that Debbie was right. Paula was really dedicated to this job, and she had been very sweet about including Laura in the service training of the pledges. I don't know what's wrong with me lately, Laura said to herself as she pulled into a parking place in the hospital lot.

Chapter 5

❂•❂

*L*aura stayed at the hospital through dinner, helping deliver meals and keeping some patients company as they ate. By the time she left, she didn't feel nearly as tired as she had when she'd first arrived. Somehow, spending time there gave her energy. The other Pearls were always telling her she was a saint to put in so much time at Kenilworth Memorial, but as she'd tried to tell them repeatedly, she honestly believed that her work at the hospital had nothing to do with being good or kind. She went there because she liked going. Laura wasn't any better than anyone else, and she put so much time in at Kenilworth because she knew how rewarding it was. She received much more from her work than she gave. Laura's one big regret was that her knowledge was so limited; she knew so little that could really be of any help. Sometimes, as she left, she wished she could just make the next eight years hurry by in an instant. Then she would have already completed medical school, and she'd really be able to do something for the people who were so sick.

Laura tried to imagine herself as a doctor, but it seemed so far away that it was sometimes hard to picture. That's why she especially liked seeing Dr. Farrand, a first-year resident in pediatrics, at work. Dr. Ferrand always seemed to have an extra moment to joke with a little boy who was scared of getting his tonsils out or to hug a small girl who was undergoing chemotherapy. She seemed young and nice, and Laura hoped that one day she'd be able to emulate the resident.

Once, when Laura had been working pediatrics, Dr. Farrand had joked that Laura was there so much that people were going to think she was a permanent employee. Laura had shyly confessed to the resident that she hoped to go to medical school someday. "What is it like?" Laura had asked.

Dr. Farrand's warm brown eyes filled with a mixture of tenderness and humor. "Well, I won't tell you it's easy, Laura. It's not. It's one of the hardest things you'll ever do. And unfortunately there are still some men who don't think women should be doctors. And although there are less and less of them, thank heavens, it makes it extra tough. But don't let that discourage you. If you want to be a doctor, go for it. And when a little

boy like Bobby over there"—she nodded toward
the nearest bed—"is brought in here with convul-
sions and you know how to treat him, you'll know
that every all-night study session, every procedure that made you queasy the first time you saw
it, every date you gave up, was worth it."

As she often did, Laura thought of Dr. Farrand's
words when she left the hospital. Sliding into the
smooth blue leather seat of her car, Laura thought
about how lucky she was to have such supportive
parents. She wondered what most of her friends'
parents would have said about their daughters
becoming doctors. Then she smiled. That wasn't
very likely to happen. Her friends in Pearl weren't
dumb at all, but none of them seemed to care
much about grades, either.

Before she knew it, the weekend had flown by,
and half of Monday was gone as well. Jacqui, her
strikingly dark beauty highlighted by the antique
white blouse she was wearing, picked through the
lettuce at the cafeteria salad bar. Then she joined
the other girls at the Pearl table. "Know what I
just remembered?" Her lips formed a pout, and
she shuddered involuntarily. "Miss McVinnis is
going to make us do that awful chemistry experiment over again today. Ugh, you know how I hate
that class. Everything smells so awful, and I'd like
to know exactly what good anyone thinks this is
going to do me in ten years!"

Paula sighed loudly. "I know. I can't believe I
have to go in there and face that witch every day.

It's enough to give me indigestion just thinking about it." In truth, the only thing that gave Paula even greater indigestion was that she was suffering through this class while Susie Madden had been transferred into Mr. John's class and was having a very easy time of it.

Laura didn't want to say anything in front of the other girls, but when lunch was over, she caught up with Paula as they walked toward class. "Paula, do you want me to go over the steps on how to find that unknown with you before we start?"

Paula gave Laura one of her most angelic smiles. "Actually, I'd rather have you just let me see your answer before you turn it in."

"Paula, you know that Miss McVinnis never gives everyone the same unknown." Laura sighed. "Look, you can't just ignore her, you know. She's going to flunk you, Paula, and what will your mom—"

Paula cut her off. "Thanks, but don't worry about it. I don't really care what my mom thinks anymore. She only worries about herself, so why shouldn't I worry about me?"

Laura shook her head, and inwardly she ached for Paula. It would be so much easier if Paula could only forgive her parents for getting divorced. And Laura knew that Paula was wrong about her mother. Just by looking at Mrs. Parker with Paula, you could tell how much she loved her daughter—and how much Paula's anger hurt her.

A few minutes later, Laura took her seat in chemistry. A tall figure sauntered by her desk.

"Looks like our lab partners are back today," a deep voice said. "I guess we don't get a second chance."

Brad didn't wait for a response. With a deliberately casual shrug, he walked toward his desk. Before Laura could decide how to respond, the bell rang.

Miss McVinnis, looking as stern as ever, suggested to the class that they attempt to use the brains that God had so graciously given them and at least try to find the right answer. "I would advise you not to waste any more time. Gene and Angie—you two will work together at lab station twelve. Brad and Laura, you will see me at my desk immediately after I dismiss everyone else to do this experiment. Are there any questions?"

Paula raised her hand, and Laura held her breath. She hoped Paula hadn't decided this was the day to take a stand against her teacher. "Miss McVinnis—" Her voice dripped honey. "Uh, could you please tell us if we'll all be working on the same unknown?"

"Why does that matter?" The way the words came out, it was clear that Miss McVinnis already knew Paula's reason, but Paula didn't flinch.

"Well, it just seems that it would be fairer that way. Otherwise, some people will have harder assignments than others."

Miss McVinnis fixed Paula with a steely glance. "Miss Parker, may I suggest that you first try passing chemistry. Then you may try teaching it. Now, everyone get to work."

Paula blushed such a deep scarlet that even the part in her long golden hair showed red. Laura knew that her sorority sister's rage was boiling just below the surface, but just then there was nothing she could do about it. Besides, Laura had enough trouble of her own. Getting called to Miss McVinnis's desk did not sound as if it could be anything good.

As they approached the teacher's desk, Brad winked at Laura. His head was held high, and she couldn't help but smile to herself. Miss McVinnis worked so hard at being ferocious, but Brad didn't seem to be the least bit intimidated.

Miss McVinnis took off her glasses, polished them, and then placed them back on her nose. Clearing her throat, she picked up the paper that they had turned in the week before. "You two," she said in measured tones, "are the only ones in this entire class who even have a clue as to what I am talking about. Therefore, you might as well work together. Oh, and since you got it right, there's no point in repeating the same experiment again. I've given you something a little more unique. Go over to lab station ten."

No one got compliments from Miss McVinnis, and in a state of shock, the two students stood before her desk even after they were dismissed. "Well, go on," said the teacher. "You can't rest on yesterday's laurels."

When they got to their lab station, Brad said, "This couldn't have worked out any better if I'd planned it myself. You know, maybe Miss McVinnis isn't all bad."

Laura felt that same twisting kind of emotion she'd felt before when she'd worked with Brad. She covered her confusion by teasing. "You're only saying that because you think I can help you get the next experiment right."

"Well, of course. What other reason could there possibly be?" he said as he reached for a beaker. His arm casually brushed across her shoulder.

Miss McVinnis had really given them a hard unknown. Nothing was falling into any sort of pattern. Brad was no longer flirting—instead, his strong jaw was set in firm concentration. "I'm not letting this thing defeat me. Maybe, if we try—" He let his words dangle in midair and reached for the bottle on the shelf above him.

Miss McVinnis had already called for everyone to clean up. In fact, the bell had just rung as Brad's extraordinary eyes glowed. "We did it. I just know we did it." He reached out his hand, caught Laura's, and raised it in victory.

"Miss McVinnis," he called with authority, "this was pretty sneaky, but we didn't get tricked. We solved your unknown!"

If they'd expected the teacher to turn cartwheels, they were mistaken. Staying right in character, she said without the slightest trace of emotion, "You'd better get your lab station cleaned up quickly or you'll receive a tardy in your next class." With that she rose from her desk and came over to look at their paper.

"It's not correct," she said, staring at the paper through her glasses, "but it's close." Then she did a most extraordinary thing. Miss McVinnis almost smiled as she said, "Oh, go ahead and go to your next class. I'll finish cleaning up the lab."

In a state of shock, Brad and Laura hurried off to their next class. Laura was still amazed by what had happened when school was over. She decided that it had been such a perfect day that the only way to make it better would be to go in and work for a while at the hospital.

It was a beautiful afternoon, and Laura was glad she had all the windows open and the radio on. The car even seemed to go to the hospital by itself, as if it were on automatic pilot and already knew the way there. Checking in at the desk, Laura was greeted warmly by JoAnn, the woman in charge of volunteer workers. "Well, let's see," she said, punching some commands into the computer. "The patient supply cart hasn't been taken to the third, fourth, or fifth floors. What would you think about doing that?"

Laura smiled. "You've got it." She put on one of the green jackets labeled "Kenilworth Memorial Hospital: Volunteer" and headed out of the office. Laura laughed to herself as she remembered the time Jacqui had confided to her that the reason she hated to work at the hospital was because of "those awful green jackets." Laura could almost hear Jacqui's exact words. "I mean, that color is the worst on me. And they have absolutely no style."

Entering the gift shop, Laura waved to the lady who ran it. "Hi, I'm here to get the patient cart." She knew the routine well. Making sure that the cart was stocked with a variety of items, she signed the inventory-control sheet, got a fair amount of change, and started down the hallway. The elevators were slow that day, and while she waited, Laura waved to many of the staff members she'd come to know.

Finally, the elevator came, and a few minutes later, it deposited her on the third floor. Laura checked in with the head nurse. "Oh, I'm so glad you made it in. Several patients have been asking me if the cart is coming around today. You must know how much it means to the people who can't move around much to have this supply cart arrive." Just then a phone rang, and the nurse rushed off to answer it.

Laura started down the hall. The third floor was filled with postoperative patients—most of the people there would be up and about soon. "Well," said the first man whose room she entered, "what have you got today?"

"There are combs and toothbrushes and things like that. But I've also brought some of the best-selling paperback books and some new magazines and some crossword puzzles and playing cards."

Laura never rushed any of the patients in their decisions. And she didn't mind if they browsed and browsed and then bought nothing at all. Realizing that for many people it was their only social activity of the day, she made sure to let them make it last.

When she got to the fourth floor, an elderly woman who'd been in the hospital for almost two months was sitting up in bed waiting for her. "When the nurse told me you were coming, I had her fix my hair. I like you. You know, I don't like that other girl who brings the cart around; she always rushes me so much."

The old woman half looked at some of the books and then told Laura a story about how she had once gone turkey hunting and killed and cleaned her own wild turkey. "I wasn't always the wreck I am now!" she finished.

"You're not a wreck at all, Mrs. Walker. You're a very interesting lady. I'll come back to see you again soon." Finally, she had finished the fourth floor, and standing at the elevator, she was ready to deal with the patients on the fifth floor.

Funny, Laura thought, there was a time when I didn't think I could ever set foot on this floor again. Now I spend the most time of all here. She wheeled the cart into the first room. A small girl who was bald from the effects of chemotherapy smiled weakly at her.

By the time she finally returned the cart to the storeroom, more than two hours had passed. She reinventoried it and turned in her sheets. Glancing at the small gold watch on her wrist, Laura decided that she had time to work another half hour and still make it home in time for dinner. She stopped by the volunteer desk again.

"I've still got a little free time," she told JoAnn. "Is there anything else that needs to be done?"

"Well," said JoAnn, "the head nurse on three just called down and asked if we had a runner available to deliver some X rays for her."

"I'm on my way," Laura said. At the third-floor nurses' station, she picked up a large stack of X rays in big brown envelopes and headed downstairs toward the X-ray lab with them. As she approached the lab, she realized that she hadn't been in this part of the hospital in quite some time. Entering the room, she saw a white-coated technician in front of a lighted screen. "Excuse me," she said, "but I brought these from—"

The figure turned, and Laura interrupted herself. "Brad! What are you doing here?"

For just an instant, Brad lost his self-assured composure and stood there, speechless. Awkwardly, he cleared his throat. "Well, I, uh—" He stared at her with a sudden look of pride in his eyes. "I plan to be a doctor someday, and I figured it couldn't hurt to find out what it was all about." Brad motioned toward the lighted screen over which two X rays were tacked. "Really, all I'm supposed to do is file and label, but some of the radiologists are really nice. They let me stand in while they read the X rays. I've learned a lot." He shrugged and smiled apologetically. "Well, this probably isn't too interesting to a girl from Pearl on a mission of mercy for her service badge."

Brad had hit not one but two sensitive spots. "Oh, come on, Brad. That's not fair," she protested. "All of the Pearls have helped out a lot here, so there's no reason to make fun of them. Besides, why wouldn't I find the hospital interesting? Maybe I plan to become a doctor, too!"

"Do you?" Brad asked in surprise.

Laura hadn't really meant for their conversation to get personal—in fact, she couldn't believe she'd shared her secret with Brad—but there was no way out of it now. "Yes," she said quietly, "I really do. That's why I worry so much about doing well in chemistry."

Brad brushed a lock of blond hair from his forehead. "Yeah, good old Miss McVinnis—which reminds me. Today it's official. You owe me a Coke." He looked at the clock on the wall. "I'll tell you what. It's almost dinnertime—if you buy me the Coke, I'll treat you to dinner at the hospital cafeteria."

Laura laughed in spite of herself. "I've been asked to some pretty fancy places before, but none of them quite compare to the hospital cafeteria."

Brad took the X rays off the screen and filed them away. "I can believe that," he said, grinning.

Laura called her parents to say she wouldn't be home for dinner and met Brad in the cafeteria line. Three hours later, long after everyone else had left, Laura and Brad were still deep in conversation. As she got into her car to drive home, Laura thought about how quickly the time had passed. It was amazing how many of the same dreams and goals they shared, and she talked eagerly, since medicine was a topic that didn't interest many of the Pearls. She'd been just about ready to leave when Brad had raised an eyebrow and said, "I think we hardworking premed students need a break. How about going to the Taft Club party with me this weekend?"

"Sure, okay." As soon as she said them, Laura couldn't believe the words that had just come out of her mouth. Feeling suddenly shy, she said a quick good-bye to Brad and headed for the parking lot. As she drove home, Laura tried not to think about the fact that she had just agreed to her first real date since Michael.

Chapter 6

Ⓞ•Ⓞ•Ⓞ

*T*he week had gotten off to a very interesting start, and it was Wednesday before Laura knew it. That evening, she was getting ready to go to the pledge meeting at Paula's house, and she suddenly wished she knew the pledges a little better. Laura hoped her speech about working at the hospital would inspire them to want to work there instead of just doing it to fulfill their pledge requirements. Pulling up in front of Paula's house, Laura saw Paula's mother leaving and stopped to say hello. Mrs. Parker looked a little tired, but she smiled and waved a greeting back. Again, Laura felt sorry for Paula and her mother—if only Paula would give her a chance. Actually, Paula said almost nothing about her mother, but even her most casual comments were tinged with bitterness about her parents' divorce. Laura shook her head sadly.

Hearing that the meeting had already started, Laura went into the house quietly and stood in the hall, waiting for a good time to walk into the meeting without interrupting it. Paula was talking, and it was impossible not to overhear her words. "Believe me, I am your best friend during the time you are pledges in this sorority. If you've got a problem, a complaint, if you're confused or even if you've got a compliment, you come to me with it. I'll handle whatever it is for you. Now, I've outlined the duties that you'll be expected to do. Anyone have any questions?"

Laura heard one of the pledges ask, "Why do they want us to have a boy walk us from class to class on Wednesday? How will that make us better Pearls?"

Paula's voice had a steel edge as she answered, "Molly, you don't question her motives when an active tells you to do something. You just do it. If and when you finally get to be an active, you'll understand why.

"Now," Paula said, turning to the entire group, "in addition to the daily activities we've planned for you, you will need to come up with a pledge prank of your own that you must plan and carry out successfully. The Pearls don't have to take you as an active until they think you've pulled off a prank that shows a high level of imagination and unity among the pledges. And it's supposed to be a complete surprise to the actives until after you've accomplished it. I'll start entertaining ideas at our next meeting."

Laura smiled at herself at the earnest tone in Paula's voice; she might be just a little too involved in training the pledges, but she certainly seemed to be enjoying it. Then Laura guiltily realized she'd been standing in the hall eavesdropping for almost five minutes. It didn't appear that Paula had noticed her entrance or had planned to stop her presentation, so Laura walked into the room.

"Laura—" Paula seemed momentarily flustered. "I guess I didn't hear you come in."

"I'm sorry I'm late," Laura replied, thinking that Paula looked especially angelic standing there in a peach cashmere turtleneck and white stirrup pants.

"Well, I guess I'll turn the pledges over to you," Paula said with a note of regret in her voice. Laura was tempted to say that she'd give them right back. Walking to the front of the room, Laura smiled at the new girls. Most of them still looked both scared and amazed to have been invited into such a select group. How well she remembered the days before invitations to pledge had been given out, when she was a freshman. There was an air of tension in the whole class. It was as if the girls felt their whole future were resting on receiving an invitation from the right sorority. In a way, it was funny; Laura had never felt the desperate desire to be a Pearl that most freshman girls feel. But on the other hand, it had never really occurred to her that she might be left out. Both Ellen and Debbie had said that it was something they had to do to make high school right. And Laura couldn't have imagined not being with her two best friends, so she had joined the rush, too.

She shook her head thinking of some of the dumb things her pledge class had had to do. Still, she'd made a lot of new friends, and there'd been no real harm done by the silly pledge activities. On the whole, she was glad that she'd joined, and especially glad to have had the opportunity to expand the Pearls' service role at Kenilworth Memorial.

She stood in front of the newest pledges and began to speak about working at the hospital. At first there was a nervous stiffness in her voice. But it quickly gave way to her excitement about what it was like at the hospital, and she talked for a little longer than she'd planned. At the end, she'd turned to Paula. "Do you want to keep track of their hours at the hospital, or do you want the pledges to turn them in to me?"

Paula immediately said, "Laura, you do such an outstanding job with the hospital that I wouldn't dream of interfering. Why don't you keep track and give the information to me?" Paula rose from the chair she'd taken in the back of the room. "Well, listen, I don't want to tie up your evening or anything. Thanks for dropping by."

Laura ignored the moment of regret she felt at not being able to stay and get to know the pledges better and graciously left. She had been home just a little over an hour when the phone rang. She answered it.

"Hi, Laura," Susie said. "I wasn't sure you'd be home yet, but I thought I'd try, anyway. Did you make it to the pledge meeting at Paula's?"

Laura could just imagine Susie smoothing out an imaginary wrinkle on her bedspread as she talked. In Susie's life, everything had its place except Paula. As president, Susie was genuinely concerned about the pledges, but as Paula's rival, there was no way she was going to call her to find out about the first meeting.

"Actually, I've been home for quite a while. I talked about the hospital, and then I left. But from what I saw, I think the pledges are off to a good start. They seem both scared and enthusiastic."

There was a hint of disappointment in Susie's voice. "Oh, I thought that as long as you were there, you might stay for the whole meeting."

Laura pulled the phone cord toward her and sat down on her bed. "Well, to tell you the truth, I probably would have stayed, but I think Paula was anxious to establish her leadership with the pledges. After all, it was their first meeting."

"You don't think she'll overdo it, do you?" There was a note of real concern in Susie's voice.

"I'm sure she'll do a good job," Laura said in a reassuring voice. She'd already decided that there was no point in inflaming an already difficult situation between her two sorority sisters.

Susie abruptly changed the subject. "Hey, I heard

that you're going to the Taft party this weekend with Brad Johnson."

Laura gripped the phone a little tighter. She should have known how fast the news would spread. "That's right," she said, trying to keep her voice calm.

"Well, I just want you to know that I'm really happy for you. He sure is cute. I think a lot of the girls have had an eye on him since he transferred here. And Laura"—her voice turned more serious— "I'm sure that a lot of guys will want to ask you out now that you're going to date again."

Laura didn't know what to say. Finally, she asked, "Isn't the party at Mike's house?"

"Sure is. And if you can believe it, the guys are even planning to serve dinner. But you'll never believe this—Mike's mom told him that their cook would have to do the barbecuing, because she didn't want the backyard burned down."

Laura chuckled and hung up the phone. She thought for a moment about how happy Susie sounded when she talked about Mike. They'd had some problems, although Susie had never confided in Laura about exactly what they were. However, everything seemed to have worked out.

The rest of the week was over before Laura knew it, and Brad was at her door on Saturday night. It was ironic that she felt more awkward that night about going to a Taft Club party with a date than she'd felt going without one for the past two years. Brad's eyes swept over her approvingly as he opened her car door, taking in her baby-blue sweater and white wool pants. The tone in his voice was light as he said, "That color definitely looks better on you than those green hospital jackets."

After that, the conversation turned to things at the hospital, and the momentary awkwardness she'd felt disappeared. Because the evening was crisp and cool, the Taft Club had built a bonfire in one corner of the Mitchells' vast backyard. The steaks from the barbecue tasted even better than they smelled. Suddenly, Laura realized that it was already eleven o'clock, although it seemed as if the evening had just begun. Inside, she felt a certain tingling—an excitement—that she hadn't felt for a long time. Brad went over to help some of the other guys pull the barbecues onto the patio, and Laura decided that it would be a good time to go inside and check her hair and makeup. The lights inside the house seemed blinding after the semidarkness of the lanterns outside. Squinting, she made her way through the living room and down what she thought was the hallway to the bathroom. The house was vast, and Laura realized that she had made a wrong turn. She was just about to go back when she heard someone crying. Following the sobs to their source, Laura saw Molly Gold sitting in a room by herself with her head in her hands. Aside from the fact that Laura hated to see anyone as upset as Molly looked, she was one of their new pledges, and Laura knew she had to see if she could help her out. Laura realized that Molly hadn't even realized that she'd come in. She bent over and gently put a hand on Molly's shoulder. "Is there anything I can do?"

Instead of looking more reassured, Molly's big brown eyes opened as if she'd seen something terrible. "Oh, no, I can't talk to you about it." She flushed a deep shade of scarlet and appeared to shrink farther into herself.

Laura's heart went out to the girl. Perhaps one of the other pledges was causing trouble and Molly was afraid to tell an active, Laura thought. "Well, then, maybe I could get Paula. Maybe you could tell her."

Hearing Laura's suggestion, Molly laughed through her tears. "No, don't do that. Paula's the last person I want to see right now. And please don't say anything to her about this. Promise me that you won't."

Laura felt helpless. "All right, I promise. But try not to be so upset," she urged, wondering what had made Molly so sad. "Is one of the Taft guys giving you a hard time?"

Molly shook her head. Biting her lip, she said, "I'll be okay; really I will. I'm sorry I bothered you."

"It's no bother," Laura said. "Are you sure there isn't something I can do for you?"

"Yes," replied Molly timidly. "If you really want to help me, just forget we had this whole conversation. If you tell anyone, I'll never get to go active."

Laura gave her word and encouraged Molly to come back out to the party with her. "I will in a minute," Molly replied. "You go ahead. Really." Respecting Molly's wishes, Laura left the room. She found the bathroom, checked her lipstick, then started back toward the party. On her way she passed Paula, hesitated for a moment, and then turned and followed her.

"Paula," she said, catching up to her sorority sister. She was still trying to figure out how she could help Molly without betraying her promise not to tell anyone what had just happened. "Have you seen Molly Gold?"

A frown creased Paula's perfect face. "Unfortunately, yes. You know," Paula said in a hushed tone, "I'm not so sure we should have invited her to join. She definitely needs to learn her place as a pledge. All she ever does is challenge what I say."

Laura felt a gnawing sense of dread growing in the pit of her stomach. "Oh, Paula," she said, "we're all friends. I mean, you don't really think that pledges are really inferior to actives, do you? Especially when we're all at parties and stuff."

Paula's blue eyes showed no emotion. "Did Molly say something to you that's bothering you?"

"No," replied Laura truthfully, "should she have?"

Paula smiled automatically. "Of course not. If any of the pledges have problems, they should come to me—and only me." She nodded her head decisively. "Well, I'd better hurry up. Gil might get lonely if I'm gone too long. And don't worry,

Laura; I'm sure that the pledges will be fine. In fact, I'm a lot more worried about Susie. She doesn't seem to be having a good time with Mike tonight. I certainly hope she isn't upset that I'm here with Gil."

With that, Paula turned and headed for the bathroom. Laura sighed as she watched her walk confidently down the hallway. Suddenly, Laura felt a pair of strong hands touch her lightly on her shoulders. "I thought you had deserted me."

Still wondering why Molly had been crying, Laura bit her lip. "Brad, how do the guys in the Taft Club treat their pledges?"

A flash of humor crossed his face. "Well, since I was only a pledge for three weeks, I'm probably not the best authority on the subject." He began to guide her back outside but then noticed how preoccupied she was. "What's the matter?" he asked gently. "What happened while I was putting away the barbecue?"

Laura sighed. "I don't know," she said. "I really don't. But I've got a feeling that something's wrong, and I don't know why, but I think it's going to get worse."

Brad looked perplexed. "What are you talking about?"

"Oh, nothing, I guess," Laura said, feeling suddenly foolish. She couldn't tell Brad how much she worried about Paula being pledge trainer even if she wanted to.

Paula passed the two of them on her way back outside. She smiled and waved. Laura noticed that Brad watched her go, shaking his head as Paula walked out the door. "She's pretty, isn't she?" Laura asked.

"Oh, I guess so." Brad shrugged. "But there's something about her that I don't trust." He shook his head again. "I feel sorry for anyone who gets on her bad side." He flashed Laura an inviting grin. "Actually, there's another Pearl I find much more interesting." His arm tightened around Laura's shoulder. "Let's go dance."

Chapter 7

●○●○

The sliver of a moon and twinkling torchlights provided only shadowy glimpses of the couples dancing to the soft music. For a while, Laura tried to spot Molly among the moving figures, but it was impossible. Finally, she gave up trying. Brad pulled her closer, and Laura allowed her head to rest against his shoulder.

Later, after Brad had taken her home, Laura thought with surprise that the evening had gone very smoothly. To her even greater surprise, she realized that instead of dreading Brad's goodnight kiss, she had actually enjoyed it. He'd been so tender and gentle as he'd touched his lips to hers. Now she stood at her window and opened it to look out at the stars winking brightly in the fall sky. Memories of evenings with another boy flooded into her mind. "Michael," she whispered to the darkness, "this doesn't take anything away from what we had. You know I'll never forget you."

On Monday, Brad walked Laura to her next class after chemistry; later, he stopped by the Pearl table at lunch to ask her if she'd be at the hospital that night. Some of the girls were beginning to ask Laura whether she and Brad were going out. Laura had avoided answering their questions. The question arose again as the active Pearls gathered for a Thursday-night meeting. Laura shrugged her shoulders. "He's a terrific guy, but I wouldn't say we were a couple or anything." While she had to admit to herself that the thought was not exactly displeasing, she still felt a tug of loyalty to Michael that left her uncomfortable about caring too much about anyone else.

Susie tapped her gavel three times, and the girls rose to recite the Pearl pledge and begin the meeting. She gave the president's report and was nearly finished discussing new business when Julie raised her hand. "I'd just like to say again that I think Paula is doing an incredible job with the pledges. Not all of you see how hard she's working, but I do—she's been terrific checking up on each and every one of them. Also, I know that Paula is really making sure that she checks their notebooks to make sure they have a guy walk them to their classes every Wednesday."

There were murmurs of approval throughout the room. Only Liz noticed the resentment behind Susie's smile as she joined in with the group's congratulations.

In a flush of victory, Paula went up to the front of the room to talk about the pledges. "Thanks loads for your support, you guys. I really appreciate your confidence in me. But I don't think I've done nearly enough. I want this to be the best, most unified, pledge class ever. I've even told them that they'd better plan a fantastic pledge prank or you'll never let them go active."

The girls all laughed. Every pledge trainer told her pledges that, and every pledge class was sure that its wonderful prank was the reason they'd been allowed to go active. Only afterward did they find out that the date for going active was set when the girls first pledged—the prank had nothing to do with it.

"Anyway," Paula continued, "I think there's still a lot to be done in the next few weeks. In fact, I have a great idea that I wanted to bring up at this meeting. It will help them understand how much they'll have to depend on one another in order to come up with a good prank. What do you think of this? Next Saturday, we take all the pledges to the bluff, line them up, and blindfold all but the first one. Then we tell them to hold on to one another's waists and find their way back to the bottom." Paula looked positively radiant. "I think that will definitely make them see the need for pledge unity."

The room was silent as the Pearls all looked at one another with questioning expressions. Paula stood before them, perplexed by the lack of comment. "So what do you think? Does someone want to make a motion in favor of taking the pledges to the bluff?"

For the first time, some of the girls realized that Paula hadn't been kidding. But still, no one said a word. Susie had been leaning against the wall, and she was the one who finally spoke up. "People might get hurt. What would happen if one of the girls fell?"

Paula said nothing, and the silence in the room was tense. Then Liz's hand shot up. "I think Susie's right. The bluff is steep and rocky. It would be too dangerous."

There were nods and mumbles of agreement. Even Julie and Monica, who always agreed with Paula, looked uncomfortable with the idea. Paula sized up the situation quickly and forced a smile to her lips. There was no reason to let herself be defeated, and it was obvious that if this were pushed to a vote, it would fail. "Well, listen, I know those pledges better than anyone, and I know nothing terrible would happen. But I certainly wouldn't want any of them getting hurt, either. I really appreciate everyone's comments, and now that I think about it, I agree with you. Thanks. And thanks again for all your compliments about the job I'm doing."

With that, Paula walked confidently back to her seat. She noted that her hands weren't shaking, which was good; it never helped anything to let people know you were angry. Still, she couldn't understand her sorority sisters. She was handling the pledges just fine—everyone said so. So why didn't they leave her alone and let her do her job? Besides, she thought defensively, if they had gone on the hike, she'd have watched over the pledges. Probably none of them would have even complained—none of them except Molly Gold, that is. Paula grimaced thinking of Molly—she was the most questioning pledge Paula had ever met. Why couldn't she just accept everything the pledge trainer said? Paula began to wonder vaguely if Susie had anything to do with all of Molly's questions. Suddenly, she realized that while she'd been absorbed by her own thoughts, the meeting had ended. Too bad, she thought, watching the girls file out of the Maddens' family room. She hadn't expected her sorority sisters to let her down so badly.

The situation didn't exactly improve at the next Pearl meeting. Susie opened it by saying that she had an important announcement to make. "Yesterday Mrs. O'Neill called a special meeting for all the sorority and fraternity presidents. She wanted to be completely sure that we knew she wouldn't tolerate anyone doing anything to school property." Susie paused. "Do you think that maybe she was a little upset about the red paint that somehow got dumped in the swimming pool last year?" Trying to suppress the grin that came to her face, Susie continued. "Anyway, she said that any sorority or fraternity that caused damage to school property would lose its status as a school-sponsored group. That would mean that it could no longer display fraternity or sorority symbols on campus, use school facilities, or participate in the fall rush." Pushing a stray strand of blond hair back from her face, she added, "We all know that that really means the end of that sorority or fraternity." Susie carefully avoided Paula's eyes as she looked around the room. "So even though we've never monitored the pledge prank before, maybe this year we should have the idea submitted to the whole group for approval. I don't really want to do that, but I'd also hate to see Pearl kicked off campus."

Paula's eyes were blazing. So that's what all this was about. Susie couldn't stand not knowing exactly what was going on with the pledges, and this was her plan to make sure she did. Well, it wasn't going to work, Paula vowed. She wouldn't let Susie get away with it. But she needn't have worried. Moments later, Becky Anderson, last year's pledge trainer, came forward. "Susie, you know Mrs. O'Neill would never kick the Pearls off campus. And besides, nothing we've ever done has really hurt property or people, and I think Paula can be trusted to make sure nothing happens this year. I like not knowing what the pledge prank is until after they've pulled it off. I move that we keep the prank secret."

A quick vote was taken, and it clearly showed that everyone wanted to preserve the secrecy of the pledge prank. Paula looked triumphant as Susie tried to save face. "Then the pledge prank will follow tradition," she said. "Let's move on to new business."

Laura raised her hand. "I want to remind everyone again to put in their hours at the hospital. Every bed is filled at Kenilworth Memorial, and the nursing staff is really overworked. I know they'd appreciate any extra time you could put in." She could tell that she didn't have their full attention. They were ready for the meeting to end.

Darn it, she thought with frustration. Why does everyone want to spend so much more time discussing pledge pranks than hospital work?

Looking on the bright side, though, Laura told herself that at least Brad was as enthusiastic about volunteering at the hospital as she was. A few nights earlier, when they'd met in the cafeteria for a Coke, he'd told her in an excited voice that he'd correctly identified a slight fracture of the tibia on an X ray of a man's leg. The doctor reading the X ray hadn't even pointed it out to him.

Laura was also glad that the pledges had been putting in so many hours at the hospital. She'd run into many of them while she was working, and it seemed to her that they were enjoying what they were doing. Suddenly, Laura remembered the pledge service hours she was keeping track of for Paula, and as Paula started to leave the room, Laura called to her. "Paula, wait a sec." Digging in her purse, she said, "Somewhere in here I have the pledge service hours for you. Oh, I

hate this purse. I can never find anything in it."
Laura dug some more. "I know it's here. Aha!"
Triumphantly, she pulled out a sheet from her
purse. "These are the pledges' hours for the past
two weeks." She unfolded the paper and held it
out to Paula. "As you can see, the pledges are
really putting in a lot of time. And Molly Gold had
the most hours again."

There was more than a hint of criticism in
Paula's voice as she said, "Well, it's nice that she
can do something right."

Laura was concerned and more than a bit curi-
ous. "You don't like Molly very much, do you?"

Paula became guarded. "Is that what she told
you?"

"No, actually, I haven't talked to her since—"
Laura had been about to bring up that night at
the Taft party, but then she remembered she'd
promised not to. "Forget it. You know, it's sur-
prising that we both spend so much time at the
hospital but we never seem to run into each
other. JoAnn, the lady who works the volunteer
desk, tells me that Molly has been doing a wonderful job."

Paula rolled her eyes in disgust, and once again
Laura wondered why she disliked Molly so much.
"Listen, Laura—" A smile had returned to Paula's
lips, and she gave her sorority sister a sincere look.
"I know I'm way behind on my hours, but honest,
keeping up with pledge activities has taken every
second of my time. As it is, I have practically no
time to even crack open the books."

Laura fidgeted with the strap on her purse. She hated any kind of confrontation, and although she'd have liked to tell Paula that everyone had to do their part at the hospital, it just didn't seem worth getting Paula upset. Besides, she reasoned silently, Paula is really working hard on sorority business, and she is barely passing her classes as it is. She doesn't need any more pressure. Laura thought of Molly and decided that she probably didn't need any more pressure either. So maybe it was just as well that Paula wasn't around the hospital very much.

Laura looked up to see her talking with Monica across the room, and realized that Paula hadn't even waited for a response. Laura stood there feeling torn. Maybe, she thought, I need to be more assertive. On the other hand, maybe I just need to be less sensitive. Paula probably just didn't think there was anything further to say about the hospital.

Chapter 8

$\mathcal{L}$*aura could hardly wait for school to be over* on Wednesday afternoon so that she could go over to the hospital. Unfortunately, it had been such a busy week that she hadn't been able to put in as many hours as usual, and she really felt the loss. She played with the perfect strand of pearls around her neck as she headed her car toward Kenilworth Memorial. Touching the necklace that symbolized her active status in the sorority, Laura realized that it wouldn't be long before the pledges would be wearing theirs. Although they didn't know it, initiation was coming in just a few weeks. Laura sighed and hoped that they wouldn't get so involved in pulling off their pledge prank that they'd forget their volunteer work.

Laura pulled her car into a space right near the

main entrance of the hospital and turned off the motor. In no time, she was checking in at the volunteer desk. JoAnn was pleased to see her. "I've missed you this week, Laura, but the other Pearls have started doing their share in the past few days, so we've had plenty of help. You must have gotten them really fired up; just look at this sign-in sheet." Laura scanned it quickly. Most of the names on it were pledges. Maybe they figured that they were close to going active and were trying to do whatever they could to make points with the older girls. On the other hand, maybe they genuinely liked donating time there. Laura hoped the latter was true.

"You're right," she told JoAnn. "The sign-in sheet is incredibly full. So, what have you got for me this afternoon?" Laura asked. JoAnn punched something into the computer.

Reading the screen, she replied, "Well, the pharmacy needs someone to repackage some pills; the cafeteria could use a hand during dinner, and oh, heavens, the patient cart hasn't been on the third floor yet today. I don't know what happened."

Laura smiled, glad that one of her favorite jobs was still available. "I'll take the patient cart up to three, then check back in with you later."

"That would be great," JoAnn said. "You know, having this computer certainly has made it easier to coordinate things. We never used to be able to use our volunteers to their fullest because it was so hard to keep track of what needed to be done.

But now, whoever needs help just punches it into the computer. I can coordinate our whole volunteer staff in seconds."

Laura said good-bye to JoAnn and headed for the gift shop to get the patient cart. On her way, she thought about how complicated things must have been before they had gotten the computer. Proudly, she remembered that it had been her mother's auxiliary group that had raised the funds to buy the computer system for the hospital.

When she reached the gift shop, Laura found that the cart had never been unloaded after it had been taken to the other floors. It took her only a minute to do a quick inventory and head up to the third floor. Knowing that she had only one floor to cover that night, Laura took her time. She stopped even longer than usual to chat with the patients. When one man wanted to buy a magazine but didn't because the medication he'd been given made him too dizzy to read, Laura offered to read a couple of articles aloud to him. She was touched to see how grateful he was.

Just as she was finishing taking the cart around, a nurse called her over to the desk. "Hi, Laura," she said. "I hope you still have a Milky Way on that cart, because I have a real craving for one. I don't get a break for two more hours, or I'd go downstairs and get one myself."

"Well," Laura replied, "I did have some here. But only a few of the patients were on restricted diets today, and I sold a lot of candy." The two of them searched the cart carefully, but there were no Milky Ways anywhere. "I'll tell you what," Laura offered. "I was just on my way back to the gift shop to return the cart. I'll pick up a Milky Way while I'm down there and bring it back to you."

"Oh, I couldn't ask you to do that," the nurse protested.

"You didn't ask," Laura reminded her. "I offered. And it's really no problem at all." With that, Laura started to wheel the cart to the elevator. "I'll be back," she promised, "Milky Way in hand."

The lady in the gift shop was just getting ready to close it for the evening and was glad to see Laura had returned. "I was just about to send a search party out for you," she teased. "How many floors did you do?"

"Just one," Laura said with a blush. "I'll inventory this real fast." She quickly counted up what she'd sold, turned in the money she'd been paid, and bought a Milky Way on her way out the door. Crossing the lobby to the elevators, she heard her own stomach grumble and decided that she'd better think about getting dinner for herself. Maybe she'd even stop by the X-ray lab and see if Brad was available to join her. The thought brought a smile to her lips.

After waiting for a few minutes, Laura decided to forget about taking the elevators. They were moving exceptionally slowly, and the staircase was nearby. Feeling content with the way the afternoon had gone, she took the steps two at a time. At first, Laura didn't see the girl who was sitting with her head in her hands on the landing of the second floor. In fact, she went flying past her, but then turned and stopped. "Molly?" she said tentatively. "Is that you?"

Molly looked up and bit her lip. Her eyes were swollen, and it was obvious that she had been crying. To cover her embarrassment, she tried to joke. "It seems like this is the only way you ever see me. Believe it or not, sometimes I do smile."

Laura dropped the Milky Way she was holding into the large pocket of her jacket. She didn't want to pry or seem too nosy, but she couldn't just leave Molly there. Besides, Laura still felt guilty for not making sure Molly was okay after the incident at the Mitchells' party; she'd never even found out why Molly had been so upset. She sat down on the step next to Molly. "Actually, I've been meaning to call you to thank you for putting in so much time here. You've given more hours than any other pledge."

Molly pulled her long brown hair back behind her and stared straight ahead. "You don't have to thank me, because I don't think I'm coming back anymore." She sighed sadly. "You know, in a way it's almost funny—working here was the thing I liked best about being a Pearl pledge, but even this didn't work out."

"Why? Molly, what happened?"

The girl's tone was flat as she spoke. "Do you ever work much on the fifth floor?"

Laura gasped, but then she realized that Molly couldn't possibly know about Michael. Lost in her own thoughts, Molly hadn't even noticed Laura's reaction. She continued talking, more as if to sort out her own feelings than to give any explanations to Laura.

"Her name was Sandra," Molly said. "She had the biggest blue eyes you could ever imagine, and she never complained. They took her in for chemotherapy, and her hair fell out. It also made her sick to her stomach, but she kept believing that she was going to get well. I guess I believed it, too. She had this Cabbage Patch doll named Elizabeth Ann, and when Sandra was really weak, she'd ask me to dress and undress Elizabeth Ann and make her talk to her.

"Last week I missed a pledge meeting because as I was getting ready to leave the hospital, Sandra asked me if I wouldn't stay and feed Elizabeth Ann her dinner. We pretended that Elizabeth Ann had refused to eat her vegetables, and Sandra giggled and told her she had to do it."

Molly shook her head slowly. "Boy, was Paula ever furious with me for missing that meeting, especially when I wouldn't tell her why." Molly turned to face Laura. "Can you just see me telling Paula that I couldn't come because I was playing dolls with a seven-year-old?" A small smile broke through Molly's tears at the thought.

"Anyway, I didn't mean to get so attached to Sandra. One day, when I first signed in to work, JoAnn asked me if I'd read stories to the kids. I'm in the drama club at school, and reading didn't seem like much work. It was fun. That's where I met Sandra." Molly's voice dropped to a whisper. "Oh, Laura, when I got to the hospital today, the first thing I did was run upstairs to check on her. When I got to her room, they told me she was gone ... only they didn't mean that she'd gone home." Molly choked back a sob and buried her face in her hands again. "I don't want to work here ever again."

Laura felt her own tears rolling down her cheeks. All of the painful memories of those last few weeks with Michael came flooding back to her. "Molly, I know how terrible you feel, but you're wrong to decide that you'll never come back. You made things a little easier for Sandra. Isn't that worth the pain you're feeling now?"

"You don't know how much it hurts," Molly replied.

"Yes, I do." A lump rose in Laura's throat as she thought about how she'd watched her six-foot tall, athletic boyfriend grow weaker and weaker as the cancer ravaged his body. She told Molly the story. "When I met Michael, I was a freshman, just like you are now. He was a junior, a member of Taft Club, and I thought he was the most handsome boy I'd ever seen. When he first walked over to me and asked me to dance, I almost fainted. But within an hour I felt as if I'd known him all my life. From then on we were always together." Laura stopped talking for a moment, her mind lost in memories.

"When he first found out he had cancer," she continued, "we were sure he'd beat it. At worst, he'd miss the basketball season. The doctor even said that lots of people came through the kind of cancer he had. But the doctors didn't know everything. Michael just got weaker and weaker. He spent the last weeks of his life on the fifth floor of this hospital. After he died, I felt like you do now, at first. I didn't think I could ever set foot in this place again. But then I realized that it didn't do anyone any good to be bitter. By spending time here, I figured maybe I could help someone cope with being sick a little better. It was then that I made up my mind that I wanted to become a doctor. Maybe someday when a boy like Michael or a girl like Sandra goes to a hospital, I'll know what to do to make them well enough to leave again."

Molly's tears had stopped, but she didn't say anything. Laura continued. "Don't you see? That's the only hope we have. We've got to try to help each other."

Molly reached over and hugged Laura. "I think you're about the nicest person I've ever known. Somehow it does help to know that maybe my being here made things a little easier for Sandra. I'm not sure I can do it, but I'll try to have at least some of the courage you do. And, Laura, I'm so sorry about Michael. I didn't know."

"It's okay," Laura reassured her. "And don't be sorry. He was a wonderful person, and I'll never forget him. All of the wonderful times we spent together were worth the pain of losing him."

Long after Molly had left, Laura sat on the stairs, thinking about Michael. Suddenly, the two years faded away, and she could see everything as vividly as if she'd just been with him last week.

Chapter 9

*L*aura wasn't sure how long she had been sitting there when a chill swept over her and she put her icy fingers in her jacket pockets to warm them. "Oh, no," she gasped out loud as she realized she'd forgotten to bring the nurse her candy bar. Laura pulled herself to her feet and headed for the third-floor nurses' station.

The grateful nurse on the third floor greeted Laura with a smile. "I thought that you'd forgotten all about me and gone home." Then she noticed Laura's puffy eyes. "You look so pale. Are you okay?"

Laura nodded, although she didn't feel okay at all. She had a sudden desire to go up to the fifth floor, to the room that had been Michael's. She wished that somehow he'd still be there. But that wasn't something she could explain to the nurse;

in fact, it didn't even make sense to her. She had accepted Michael's death a long time ago. Trying to smile at the nurse, she said, "I'm fine. I'm just tired, I guess. Oh, and I'm really sorry for taking so long with your candy bar."

"No problem. You want half? You look as if you could use a little treat," the nurse commented.

But Laura wasn't hungry anymore. In fact, she didn't think she could have eaten right then if she had to. She said good-bye to the nurse and started down the hallway, still feeling the unsettling tug of Michael's presence all around her. I'll just go home and take a hot bath. That will make me feel better, Laura told herself as she stopped in the rest room to wash her face and apply some fresh lipstick. Suddenly, she felt too drained to walk down three flights of stairs, so she waited for the elevator.

Reaching the lobby, she headed quickly toward the front doors of Kenilworth Memorial and the parking lot that lay beyond them. "Hey, Laura," came a strong, masculine voice. She stopped where she was standing and turned around.

Brad moved toward her with strong, positive strides. "I've been looking all over for you. I even checked the parking lot to make sure your car was still here. I wanted to know if you'd have dinner with me. I'll even treat you to the Hamburger Hamlet instead of the hospital's cafeteria food."

Laura tried to smile. She was glad that she'd washed her face and fixed her makeup; if she hadn't, Brad would have asked a lot of questions that she didn't want to answer. "It sounds like a terrific invitation," she said, hoping she sounded enthusiastic, "but actually I'm just beat. Could we do it some other time?"

The concern in Brad's eyes was obvious. "Okay. I hope you feel better. Hey, how about if we have dinner on Saturday instead?"

Suddenly it seemed to Laura as if Michael were standing right there next to her. She couldn't even meet Brad's eyes as she said, "I don't think so. I, uh, I don't know." Realizing how rude she must sound, she added, "I'll let you know. I just need to go home right now."

"Listen," Brad said, his arm slipping protectively around her shoulder, "how about if I drop you off at home and we can pick up your car tomorrow?"

Laura couldn't meet Brad's probing look, but with false cheeriness she answered, "I'm fine. Really I am. I just need some sleep. I'll talk to you tomorrow at school."

Arriving home, she decided to skip her planned bath and go to sleep. She climbed into bed, still thinking of Michael. At the end, she'd wanted to be so strong for him, but she'd been so lost in her own grief that she couldn't. As sick as he had been, Michael had still recognized her pain. He'd motioned her over to his bedside and taken her hand. "It'll be okay, Laura. I'm not afraid of dying anymore. But I am worried about you. Promise me," he'd said with an urgent look in his eyes.

"Promise me that you won't sit around feeling sad after I'm gone. Make the most of your life. You have to, because now you know how special life is. Besides, it will make it easier for me if I know that you'll have enough adventures, enough excitement and fun, for both of us. Be with our friends, go to their parties, listen to their secrets, and know that a part of me will always be there, too."

Laura had promised, and she'd tried to keep that promise. Her friends said how brave she was to continue with all of her activities after Michael had died. But they didn't understand. It wasn't that she didn't feel like hiding somewhere and crying; it was just that she knew that she was doing what Michael had wanted her to do the most.

Laura lay in bed and dabbed away her tears. Her talk with Molly had taken much more out of her than Laura had realized. Finally, she fell asleep, but her dreams were troubled. She dreamed she was at a carnival with Michael and they were on a Ferris wheel. She was laughing, and he kissed her tenderly as the Ferris wheel turned high up in the sky. But then, when she got off, he was no longer with her. She walked through the fair grounds, looking for him, but she couldn't find him. She saw no one that she knew until she got to the roller coaster. Brad was in the front seat, and he called to her to join him. "I can't," she called, but he couldn't or wouldn't hear her.

"Come on! You'll miss all the fun!" Brad's voice

shouted into the wind. Colored lights blinked on and off, and there was a ringing sound as the roller coaster took off down the track.

As the ringing sound continued, Laura realized that it was not the starting bell of a roller coaster but her alarm. She woke up feeling as if she'd barely slept at all. Laura sat up in bed, feeling shaky and looking gratefully around her room to reassure herself that everything had just been a dream. After her restless night, there was something almost comforting about getting ready for school the same way she did every day. Even Mrs. Alexander's boring history lecture seemed somehow reassuring.

Laura unfolded the note that Debbie had passed to her in French class: *I've got to talk to you at lunch. Big problems. Paula.* Even without the signature, Laura would have recognized Paula's perfect script. She also noticed that the word "big" was underlined three times, and a frown creased her forehead. It's got to be about Molly, Laura decided. But what? Maybe Paula started in on her today and Molly depledged. Laura bit her lip. It was entirely possible, but Paula probably wouldn't consider Molly's refusing to join Pearl a problem. Unless, of course, some of the other girls had depledged with her. Laura began to wonder if there was any way she could get to Molly before lunchtime. She had finally gained the younger girl's trust last night, and Laura hated to think she might lose it by appearing to side with Paula.

The problem was that it was already third hour; they only had one more class before lunch. Laura had no idea where Molly's classes were. Somehow she'd have to get the information from attendance, then track Molly down, and still not be late for her next class. Laura absently ran her hand through her curls. That wouldn't work. One more lateness in English and Mrs. Fields would absolutely kill her. Well, maybe I could check after fourth hour, before I go to lunch, she decided.

"Mademoiselle Clark, can you or can you not conjugate the verb *manger* in the past perfect?"

"I, uh, I—" Laura gulped and tried to get her mind back to French. "I'm sorry, Mme. Roese. I wasn't paying attention." She forced herself to concentrate on French for the rest of the hour. Once or twice during English class, she let her thoughts wander back to Molly and Paula. She hoped she could catch Molly before lunch. Laura watched the clock and began gathering her books a few minutes before the bell rang to make sure that she would be the first one out of the class. But Mrs. Fields had other plans.

"Oh," the English teacher said when the bell rang, "stay right where you are. I still have to give you your vocabulary assignment." Reluctantly, Laura opened her notebook to take down the added assignment. By the time she gathered her books again, the hallways were already crowded with people. Laura began to push her way toward the attendance office when she heard a voice call to her.

"Laura, did you get my note?" Paula fell in step with her. "I gave it to Julie, who said she'd give it to Ellen, who said she'd give the note to Debbie to give to you in third hour. But I was still worried that you might not get it!"

Laura looked longingly toward the attendance office. Well, it's too late for that, she thought regretfully. Somehow I'll have to try to help Paula without betraying Molly. Laura had to admit that Paula's angelic blue eyes looked quite troubled as she nervously pulled at several strands of her long blond hair. Trying to make Paula feel a little more at ease, Laura answered, "Well, you shouldn't have worried. The Pearl delivery system came through perfectly. What's up?"

Paula sighed deeply. "Laura, it's so awful. Listen, I don't want anyone else to know, so go get your lunch and then bring it outside to eat. I'll meet you there."

"What about your lunch?" Laura asked.

"Oh, I couldn't possibly eat. I'm much too upset."

"Well," Laura said, "then my lunch can wait, too. Let's go sit in the breezeway near my locker—no one's usually out there. I'll do whatever I can to help you." Laura felt a pang of guilt at her words and tried to reassure herself that her comment did not mean that she was taking Paula's side.

Paula's face began to brighten. "Thanks, Laura. I knew I could count on you. I just knew it." The two girls sat down on the cool tile in the glass-enclosed walkway. Laura decided that if she had to, she'd just tell Paula that she couldn't count on her if it meant hurting someone else. She'd be a good sorority sister, but not at Molly's expense. Laura just hoped she could smooth things over.

Paula glanced at her watch. "We don't have much time, so I'll fill you in fast. I was walking through the north hallway before school this morning when Miss McVinnis—the dragon lady—came out from her cage. I pretended that I didn't even see her; I mean, why pay any attention to that awful witch for one minute outside of chemistry, right?" Without waiting for any answer, she continued. "But she saw me and called me into the lab." Paula shuddered. "I thought about not going—anyway, to make a long story short, she had the nerve to tell me that I was an absolute disgrace as a student. She said she was appalled by my lack of effort. Anyway, she just wanted me to know that if I didn't pass the test today, I would fail her class. Laura, I knew I wasn't exactly getting A's, but failing? My mother will kill me." Paula grimaced and spoke bitterly. "She said that if I didn't pass all my classes, she'd forbid me to participate in any Pearl activities for a month. Can you see me missing the initiation of my own pledges? Susie would certainly love that." Her large blue eyes beseeched Laura. "You've got to help me cram," she begged. "You've got to get me through this test."

"Well, I'll try," Laura said. Her head was spinning. Paula hadn't wanted to talk about Molly at all. How ironic, Laura thought to herself. I spent two hours figuring out how to handle a nonexistent problem.

Laura opened her notebook. "Okay, Paula, here goes. I mean, I'm no great chemist, but I'll do my best. I won't even try to cover everything; I'll just try to teach you a few things that I'm sure will be on the test and hope that's enough to get you through."

"Sounds good to me," said Paula. "I'm all ears."

For the next thirty minutes the two girls worked hard. But Laura knew it hadn't been enough. Paula was still totally lost. She tried to warn Paula that Miss McVinnis meant business, but since Paula had always pulled through her classes before, she hadn't paid any attention. Oh, well, thought Laura, it won't do any good to bring all that up now.

The bell rang. "Paula, I've got to get going," Laura said. "My next class is way on the other side of the building. I'll see you in chemistry. Good luck. And, remember, the valence for calcium is plus two."

Paula shook her head, looking totally defeated. "Laura, I really appreciate all your help, but I'm never going to do it. I just wish you sat near me. Maybe, if I used your paper, my brain would make it through this class."

Laura stood up and smoothed out the wrinkles in her skirt. "Oh, I don't think I'd try cheating in Miss McVinnis's class. She'd kill you if she caught you. Just have faith in yourself. I know you can do it."

"You really think so?"

Laura paused for a minute. She didn't think so, but saying she did could only give Paula a little more confidence. "You'll do it. You've never failed a class yet, have you?"

"That's true," Paula said, her face brightening a little. "Maybe I'll tell my English teacher that I need to go to the nurse this hour. That way I can study a little longer."

"Well, good luck," Laura called, rushing off to her class. When it ended, she headed quickly to chemistry, hoping she could get there in time to cover a couple of last-minute facts with Paula. But when she arrived, Laura saw to her surprise that Paula looked entirely different than she had at lunch.

She waved at Laura and smiled. "Listen, I owe you a lunch," she promised. "I'm sorry about making you miss yours this afternoon."

"It's okay. Listen, I thought of a couple of other things that will definitely be on the test."

"Forget it," Paula said. "It's probably bad luck to cram. Besides, I'm sure I'll be fine." Laura looked totally perplexed. "You should see the look on your face." Paula laughed. "I'll call you after school and tell you all about it."

Brad strode into the classroom and headed directly for Laura. "I've really been worried about you—first you were acting weird last night, and then no one saw you at lunch today."

Laura's heart fluttered at Brad's concern. "I'm fine. I really am. I only missed lunch because I was trying to help Paula do some last-minute cramming for this test. But, Brad—thanks."

The bell rang and cut off any further discussion. The difficulty of the test soon took Laura's mind away from anything but trying to answer the many complex questions.

Chapter 10

◐•◐•◐

*L*aura still wasn't finished when the bell rang, and the rest of the class had filed out by the time she handed in her test. "Laura, your time is up," said Miss McVinnis, walking over to her desk.

"I just have this one problem," Laura pleaded, and hurriedly wrote an answer. "Thanks for letting me finish."

Miss McVinnis almost smiled. "I'm pleased that you were concerned about your performance."

Laura thought about chemistry through her last class. Miss McVinnis had asked every question imaginable—the test had been six pages long! She thought she'd done okay, but it had been very hard. Even though she'd studied for almost a week, she was sure she hadn't aced the test. Laura sighed. If only good grades in chemistry weren't so important to becoming a doctor. Then she thought of Paula. There was no way Paula had passed; even if they'd had ten lunch hours, Laura wasn't sure she could have crammed enough information into Paula's head to really help her. The bell rang again, and there was an air of excitement as the students of Taft High emptied out of their classes.

Laura headed for her locker, looking for both Paula and Brad. She owe Brad an explanation for her bad behavior the day before, and Paula was definitely going to need a shoulder to cry on after the test. But it was Paula who found Laura. She waved to her as she was walking down the hallway with Bobby Brown. Laura wasn't quite sure that she believed her own eyes. Bobby Brown had been sitting next to Paula in chemistry all year, but Paula had never given him a second glance. Even so, he'd continued to stare longingly at her. Once, Laura had felt so sorry for him that she'd mentioned something to Paula about at least being friendlier to Bobby in class. Paula had only laughed and said that Laura was crazy if she thought Bobby Brown's crush was something to worry about.

Well, Laura thought as she watched them walking toward her, they definitely are a pair today.

As they approached, Laura tried to think of something to say that wouldn't come out wrong. "Hi," she finally blurted out, "I guess that we all survived chemistry. Wasn't that test something?"

"Actually," Paula said in a detached tone, "Bobby didn't think it was so bad, and you know, now that I think about it, I didn't think it was so terrible, either." She flashed an innocent-looking smile at Bobby. "Laura and I did some last-minute studying at lunch. We were a little worried."

Bobby looked awestruck to have Paula's attention, as though he wished the moment would never end. But Paula had other plans. "Listen, you two. I'd love to stay and talk, but I've got to get some pledge business done."

"Maybe I could drop you off somewhere," Bobby asked. He pushed his glasses up on his nose and stood up very straight, trying to make himself look taller than Paula.

"Oh, thanks," Paula said, "but Pearl activities are kind of secret, if you know what I mean. See ya." With that, she turned and was gone.

With a longing gaze, Bobby watched her walk away. Laura was sure that he hadn't even realized that he'd spoken out loud when he'd sighed and said, "She really is the prettiest girl at Taft." He seemed to not even realize that Laura was still there, so she slipped quietly away.

Poor guy, she thought. No wonder Paula suddenly became so unconcerned about the test. Bobby had one of the highest cumulative averages in the whole chemistry class.

On her way to the parking lot, Laura saw Paula, who waved to her and smiled. "I've got to hurry. I'm meeting with the Taft Club's pledge master to consider a joint project. But thanks for this afternoon. But after I left you, I ran into Bobby in the nurse's office. I guess you can figure out the rest."

Laura looked worried. "But Bobby—"

Paula laughed. "Laura, you worry too much. Bobby was genuinely thrilled that he could help me. And we didn't get caught cheating, so what's the problem? There was no harm done. Oops, there's Taft's pledge master. Gotta run."

Laura was still standing in the parking lot, thinking about the situation, when she felt a firm hand on her shoulder. "Are you lost, little girl?"

"Brad!" she exclaimed happily. "I'm so glad to see you."

"Well, that's nice to hear. I was beginning to wonder."

Laura blushed. The day before seemed a million years ago, and Laura suddenly realized how much she enjoyed being with Brad. "Listen," she teased, "I'm hoping that a certain person who asked me out for dinner on Saturday night hasn't forgotten that he made the offer."

Brad's blue eyes shone brightly. "Oh, I think I could probably jog his memory. In fact, I think it would be safe to say you could count on it." He looked at her long and hard, and Laura felt a pleasant chill.

"So, uh, what did you think of the chemistry test?" Laura asked, trying to hide her rising blush.

"Ychhh! That lady certainly knows how to give a hard test. I don't think your noble efforts to help Paula at the last minute were worth much. On the other hand, lunch today was an unidentifiable combination of leftovers, so you probably didn't miss much in the way of food, either."

Laura played with her watch, but she didn't say anything about her suspicion that Paula had cheated to pass the test. Noticing her gesture, Brad took her wrist and glanced at her watch. "Geez, I didn't realize how late it was! I'm going to have to run at least ten extra laps around the basketball court for being late to practice. See you later." He jogged away, but over his shoulder he called, "Don't forget about Saturday."

"I won't," Laura called back.

Friday seemed ordinarily dull, which was all right with Laura. There were no secret messages from Paula and no missed lunch hours to cram for tests. Even chemistry promised to be fairly easy. Miss McVinnis always went over some of the most frequently missed parts of each test the day afterward. That meant that Laura wouldn't have to do any labs or try to absorb any new material.

She settled into her seat and waved across the room to Brad, who winked broadly. The bell rang, and Miss McVinnis strode to the front of the room. As always, her white hair was in its impeccable bun at the back of her head, and her wire glasses were perched securely on her nose. She folded her arms across her chest, pursed her lips, and stared angrily at the class.

Laura heard the boy behind her whisper that he guessed the teacher's sour expression meant that they hadn't done very well on the test, but Miss McVinnis either didn't hear him or chose to ignore his comment. The room was absolutely still as Miss McVinnis spoke in a slow but commanding voice. "Paula Parker, will you please rise from your seat and come to the front of this classroom?"

All eyes in the room turned toward Paula, who made no effort to move. She merely stared back innocently at Miss McVinnis. "Did you want me for something?" she asked in her most ingratiating voice.

"Come here," the teacher said firmly.

Laura could almost feel Paula mentally weighing her options. Finally, she must have decided that it would be better to go. After all, Paula was positive that Miss McVinnis didn't know that she'd cheated. Laura stole a quick look in Paula's direction and saw that Bobby looked almost sick but that Paula remained as serene and angelic-looking as always. Paula rose from her chair with grace and style and walked calmly to the front of the room. She smiled at the teacher. "What can I do to help?"

Miss McVinnis, however, didn't look at Paula. Instead, she stared at the students. "You can pick up a drop slip. You've failed this class."

Paula's mouth flew open. "But that's impossible. I couldn't have failed. I know I couldn't. If I could see my paper—"

Miss McVinnis took Paula's test paper from the top of the pile on her desk. There was the sound of ripping, and then the pieces fluttered into the wastebasket. "Oh, the answers on your paper are

all right. But they didn't come from *your* brain.
And I think I've made my position about cheating
quite clear in this class. Are there any questions?"

Paula looked frantic. "Miss McVinnis, you can't
do this. Please, you just can't."

The chemistry teacher stared at her. "I didn't
do anything, Paula. You did this all by yourself."

"But you don't understand. You see, my mother—" Paula hated humiliating herself in front of
the class, but she was in a desperate situation,
and she knew she had to change Miss McVinnis's
mind now, before it got any worse.

Miss McVinnis interrupted her. "If your mother
calls, I will tell her that you are quite a capable
student. Had you studied, you could have easily
passed on your own. But obviously it was just too
beneath you to study. Now, either take this pass
slip and see about dropping the class or take
your seat. Either way, you are no longer a student
in here as far as I am concerned."

Her cheeks burning, Paula took the slip and
stormed to the door. She flung it open and then
slammed it shut as she left.

Chapter 11

❍•❍

J acqui met Laura after class. "*I think Paula's* really done it this time! Who would dare to cheat in Miss McVinnis's class? Her eagle eye doesn't miss anything. Hey, why do you suppose Paula did it, anyway? I mean, grades have never mattered all that much to Paula."

Laura's eyes clouded with worry. Jacqui obviously didn't know about Paula's mother's ultimatum. Afraid to betray her sorority sister's confidence, Laura said, "I just hope she doesn't make things worse by skipping her next class because she's so furious."

"I'd say that's a definite possibility. Paula has always been able to wheedle her way into getting a teacher to see things her way. She probably isn't all that thrilled to have been stopped dead this time." Jacqui fingered her blue ceramic beads. "I'm really worried about her."

"Hey, Jacqui," called a deep, resonant voice. Jacqui and Laura turned to see Danny Martin, and Jacqui flashed him a perfect smile. Laura could tell that Jacqui's worries about Paula were quickly fading into the background. Looking at Jacqui and Danny together, Laura was again amazed by how much she'd changed since they'd started dating. No one ever thought that one boy would be enough for Jacqui, but she'd proved them wrong. The warning bell rang, and Laura ran for her last class. As it ended, she turned her thoughts again to Paula. She was in real trouble this time, and though Laura didn't know exactly what to do to help, she hoped maybe some of her sorority sisters might have a suggestion. The only problem was that Laura couldn't tell them much. After all, Paula had told Laura in confidence about her mother's threat. Finally, Laura decided that maybe she could track Paula down by herself. Maybe she could convince Paula to let her help her.

As she started toward Paula's locker, she saw Julie across the hall. Laura motioned to her. Julie was one of Paula's best friends, and Laura decided that it could only help to have her along. Approaching Laura, Julie grinned sheepishly. "Hi, I don't blame you for wanting to talk to me. But listen—I know I owe more hours to hospital service, and I'm planning to work this weekend."

"Great, Julie," Laura replied. "But that isn't why

I wanted to talk to you. I'm trying to find Paula; have you seen her yet?"

"No, did you try looking by her locker?"

"That's where I'm heading. Why don't you come along?"

Julie looked perplexed. "Okay, but what's up?"

Laura sighed and shifted her books to her other arm. "I'll let Paula tell you, but I think she could use some friends right now."

The two Pearl sisters stood near Paula's locker and watched as the school emptied out. "I guess we must have missed her," said Julie. "Maybe you'd better tell me what's going on."

Laura bit her lip. "Let's just give her another couple of minutes. I'd really rather have her tell you yourself. And I'm sure that out of anyone, you're the person she'd want to tell."

Finally, they were the only two people left in the entire hallway, and just as they decided that Paula wasn't coming, they saw her approaching from the girls' restroom. Her normally perfect complexion was splotched with red, and her eyes were swollen and bloodshot. Julie gasped. "Paula, what's happened?"

Paula looked angry, and she bitterly intoned, "You mean the whole school doesn't know already?"

"Know what?" Julie asked, looking more perplexed than ever. Paula looked searchingly at Laura.

"I didn't say anything to anyone. Really. I just asked Julie to come with me to your locker. But,

Paula, it doesn't matter if the other girls find out. They'd just try to help you."

Paula laughed, but it was not a pleasant laugh. "Oh, Laura, quit acting like Miss Goody-Two-Shoes. I can think of tons of people who are thrilled about what happened. I'm sure Susie Madden was just brokenhearted. She'd cry all night knowing my chance to beat her for president had just been wiped away. You know, the sad thing is that I think I really would have done it. These pledges think I'm terrific." It was not a boast, just a statement of fact.

Julie looked from Laura to Paula in confusion. "Paula, for heaven's sake, will you tell me what's going on?"

"All right," she replied slowly. Julie was probably as loyal a friend as anyone had the right to expect, but Paula honestly believed that when push came to shove, people only looked out for themselves. Still, she figured, it probably wouldn't hurt to tell Julie what had happened with Miss McVinnis. It would be all over school by Monday, anyway. However, in the following split second, she decided she wouldn't tell Julie about her mother's threat to forbid her to take part in Pearl activities for a month. As a matter of fact, she wished she'd never said anything to Laura, either. Not that Laura would ever purposely hurt her—or anyone else, for that matter. But she didn't need Laura interfering, trying to make things better and messing them up altogether. She'd certainly been meddlesome enough when it had come to

Molly, and Molly was hard enough to control as it was.

"Hey," Julie said, "if you'd rather not, you don't have to say anything."

Paula pasted a pleasant look on her face. "It's okay," she said, and proceeded to tell Julie how incredibly unfair Miss McVinnis had been. She concluded by saying, "And if you can believe it, that witch didn't say a thing to Bobby. He didn't get in any trouble at all. Just me." It was as if a light had suddenly shone, and Paula's face began to brighten. "Which just may be a way for me to get out of this mess."

Laura's big brown eyes widened. "But, Paula, you know that Bobby never cheats," she argued. "He probably studied for that test for two weeks. He only tried to help you because he's been madly in love with you all semester."

"Oh, Laura, you worry too much. I've got to get out of this mess, and I can't worry about Bobby. Besides, he told me that suddenly becoming friends with me was the best thing that's happened to him in all of high school." The certainty of confidence was creeping back into Paula's voice. "Listen, I really appreciate your concern—you're both great friends—but I really think I just need to be alone to think a few things out."

Laura put her hand gently on Paula's arm. "Please," she cautioned, "think things over carefully. If you make Miss McVinnis angrier, she could get you in even more trouble."

Her long blond hair swaying behind her, Paula

put her hand over Laura's. "Don't worry; I won't. In fact, I don't think I'll ever even speak to her again. I'll work things out, though. I really will."

Julie offered again to ride home with Paula, but Paula said she'd rather be alone for a while. Julie turned to Laura. "Well, listen, I saw Debbie, and she said that a bunch of the girls were going over to Le Finis after school. Want to join them?"

"Why not?" Laura replied. "It's been quite a day."

"And don't say anything about Paula, okay?"

"Don't worry; I won't."

When they arrived at Le Finis, however, they found that they didn't have to say anything about Paula. She was already the topic of conversation. Debbie's boyfriend had been in Miss McVinnis's chemistry class, and he'd told Debbie what had happened. Jacqui had then admitted that she'd been there, too, and that it had been just horrible.

The girls squeezed closer together to make room for Julie and Laura.

"I don't think," said Susie, "that any Pearl has ever been called in front of a class and kicked out before."

Liz whistled softly. "Oh, my gosh," she said, half to herself.

"What is it, Liz?" Susie asked.

Liz wished she hadn't said anything. But now that she had, she had to continue. "Well, uh, I ran into Paula's mom at the grocery store the other day. We got talking about initiation, and she said she was very concerned about Paula's grades.

She said that maybe being pledge trainer was taking too much of Paula's time." Liz gulped. "I was just thinking that maybe the reason Paula cheated was because she was afraid her mom would make her give up being pledge trainer."

Debbie's eyes widened. "But the girls haven't done their pledge prank yet—and they haven't gone active. Now's when they need a pledge trainer most."

"Well, it wouldn't be fair to elect someone else at this point," Susie said in measured tones. "I guess as president I'd just have to finish the pledge trainer's job."

Julie shot Laura a helpless look, and Laura searched for a way to change the subject. "Well, why don't we wait and see what happens," Laura suggested. She wasn't crazy about drawing attention to herself, but it seemed the safest subject for the moment. "Hey, I'm going out with Brad tomorrow night. Does anyone know a good movie to see?"

Several suggestions were made, and then Debbie said, "Speaking of dates for tomorrow night, I've got myself in a real jam. Remember Jeff, that cousin of Bill Whiteman's who was here visiting about a month ago? Well, he's back for the weekend, and I'd really like to see him. But I've already got dates for tonight and tomorrow night that I don't want to break. So when am I going to fit Jeff in?"

Susie laughed. "Honestly, Debbie. You're worse than Jacqui was before she started dating Danny."

Debbie's smile showed that she didn't really mind the problems at all, but she said, "In a way, Susie, you're very lucky. I mean, I wish I cared about one boy the way you care about Mike." She paused meaningfully. "And maybe the way Laura is beginning to feel about Brad?"

"Oh, no," Laura said just a little bit too fast. "Brad is really just ..." Her voice trailed off. She wasn't sure how to finish the sentence.

Chapter 12

$\mathcal{S}$ome of the Pearls had planned to take a bike hike on Saturday morning. Deciding that she could use the exercise, Laura joined them. Their hour of riding had left her tired enough to look forward to a relaxed and uneventful afternoon. As she began to dress for her date with Brad, she realized that they'd never really decided what movie to see. He'd only said that he'd pick her up at seven; then they could decide what to see later. Laura thought about looking through the paper so she'd have some suggestions ready, but she decided that she really didn't care what they saw. I'll just leave it up to Brad, she thought.

Standing in front of the full-length mirror on the closet door of her bedroom, Laura examined the outfit she'd put on. Her pale pink cowl-necked angora sweater accented her dark, delicate profile, and her forest-green wool slacks suggested a hint of winter approaching. Laura applied a final touch of pink plum lipstick, giving her lips just a touch of color. Her freshly washed curls, which framed her face, shone like dark silk. "I guess I'll do," she said to herself. Almost as if on cue, Brad rang the doorbell.

He cast an approving glance at her, and his face broadened into a wide grin. Mrs. Clark walked into the hallway. "Hi, Brad," she said. "How nice you both look!"

"Thanks, Mrs. Clark," he replied. "When Laura looks this good, I have to work pretty hard just to make sure she won't be ashamed to be seen with me."

Mrs. Clark raised an eyebrow at Laura. "Watch out, honey. He's a smooth one." She winked at her daughter. "You two have a good time tonight." With that, she continued on her way into the kitchen, but Laura could tell that her mother was happy. Just the other day, her mother had mentioned what a nice young man Brad was, and her father had promptly added that any young man who got to take Laura out was darn lucky. Then he'd smiled gently at her and told her that he was glad to see that she was beginning to date again. No more had been said, and Laura knew that it wouldn't be. Her parents never pushed her, but she knew what they had been saying.

Brad settled her into his silver Saab and hopped in behind the wheel. Laura smiled at him, thinking that she really was glad the two of them were going to be together that evening. "So, where are we going?" she asked. Even though they'd been out a few times, she always felt a little awkward about breaking the ice at first.

Brad was wearing a navy sweater over a white button-down shirt, and the combination made his deep blue eyes look even more gorgeous. "Well, I had been thinking about going to that little Italian restaurant on the other side of the shopping mall. But you look so great that maybe we should go to Henry's instead. It wouldn't be fair if only a few people got to see such a beautiful girl. Okay?"

Laura giggled. "Brad, that is the most unbelievable line I've ever heard. But Henry's is fine."

Brad looked slightly contrite. "Oh, all right. So maybe it is a line, but in this case it just so happens to be true."

Laura shook her head and changed the subject. But secretly she was rather touched by Brad's glowing description. When they arrived at Henry's, they saw Susie and Mike in another booth. Mike halfheartedly invited them to join him and Susie, but Brad declined. "I'm not sharing Laura with anyone tonight!" he said. They headed toward the table that had been reserved for them.

After deciding what they wanted, they put their menus down. Brad said, "I looked for you at the hospital this morning, but I guess you didn't come in."

"I went bike riding with some of the girls this

morning. I meant to get in later, but I just never made it. Tomorrow I'll go over for a while."

Brad's eyes twinkled. "I was looking for you because the most incredible thing happened today." He began to explain how a radiologist had taken him aside and commented on his excellent mind and sharp eye. The waitress came by and took their order and then disappeared again, but neither Brad nor Laura really noticed her. Brad was totally involved in explaining how two radiologists had allowed him to listen as they consulted with each other on a hard case. "If you can believe it, when they got finished, they even took the time to ask me if I had any questions!"

Laura felt his excitement as if it were her own. Brad was the only person she knew who got as much of a thrill from the things that happened at the hospital as she did. Even her parents, who were always interested in what she had to say, weren't quite the same. They really only cared about medicine because they cared about their daughter.

As the waitress began putting their food in front of them, Brad said sheepishly, "Gosh, I'm sorry. I've really monopolized this conversation. I guess I get kind of carried away about medicine."

"Don't apologize," Laura said, her dark eyes glowing. "I feel the same way you do. Just the other night, I ran into this pledge. She had been working on the pediatric cancer floor, and she was so depressed that she didn't want to come anymore. I tried to explain to her what an incredible experience it can be to work at the hospital, what an enormous feeling of satisfaction you can get by doing something for someone else."

"Sometimes," Brad joked, "you do something for yourself, too. Isn't that where we had our first date?"

Laura smiled and picked up her fork. But inside her mind she was still replaying the rest of that conversation she'd had with Molly about Michael. Funny, she hadn't thought about it earlier, but she and Michael used to come to Henry's. Michael had liked the booth over in the right corner, the one where Susie and Mike were sitting. In some ways, Mike even looked a little like Michael, and in the dim lighting, for a minute, Laura almost thought it could be him. She gasped involuntarily and choked on a piece of salad.

"Are you okay?" Brad asked.

Laura blushed. "Fine, sorry."

"That's okay," Brad teased. "From the way you were staring at Mike and Susie, I figured you were either trying to eavesdrop on their conversation or you'd just remembered something about Mike that shook you up."

"Really," she said a shade more sharply than she had intended, "it was nothing. I'm sorry. Could you excuse me for a second?"

Brad looked a little perplexed as Laura made her way out of the booth and headed toward the ladies' room. Once inside, she gave her reflection in the mirror a stern look. Laura, you can't keep doing this to yourself, she reminded herself. You've got to promise yourself not to think about Michael when you're with Brad. She reapplied some lipstick and a smile and went back to the table.

"Sorry," she said again. "So tell me, are we going to beat Hamilton High next week in basketball?"

Brad groaned. "Are you kidding me? They're going to be a piece of cake. Even the coach thinks so. He hasn't made us come in for one extra practice."

Laura looked slightly amused. Brad would never say so himself, but rumor had it that a lot of the reason that the coach was so confident about the team had to do with a transfer student named Brad Johnson.

As they finished dinner, Brad checked his watch and said, "We'll have to get dessert later if you want it. We're a little short on time."

Laura looked confused. "Short on time? Where are we going?"

Brad grinned broadly. "Oh, it's a surprise. But don't worry; I checked it out. I'm sure it's something you'll really enjoy."

"Brad," Laura teased, "are we going back to work at the hospital tonight?"

Snapping his fingers together, Brad teased back. "Now why didn't I think of that? It would have been the perfect date." As they walked out of the restaurant, Brad reached out and caught Laura's hand in his. Laura decided it was not an entirely unpleasant feeling, although her tiny hand was totally lost within Brad's massive fingers.

"You're really not going to tell me where we're going?" Laura asked as he held the door for her.

"Nope. Ask as you will; my lips are completely locked shut."

"Well, let's see if I can guess," she said. "We're headed toward Cleremont Avenue, so that means we can't be doing anything in the mall. Will you at least tell me if we're seeing a movie?"

"Nope," said Brad, enjoying having the upper hand.

"Okay," Laura reasoned, "then how can you be so sure that I'll even like what we're doing?"

Brad chuckled heartily. "Oh, let's just say I have my sources."

Laura was a pretty good game player, but she had to admit that she was stumped. "You'll see where we're going when we get there" was all Brad would say.

Laura decided to take him at his word, and as she stole a look at his rugged profile, she decided that she was glad she'd had her little conversation with herself in the rest room. Brad was a nice person who was a lot of fun to be with. She didn't want to risk ruining what they were starting to have.

Brad pulled the car into the back lot of the Fox movie theater. "Aha," Laura cried. "So it is a movie. The only trouble is that I can't see what's playing from back here." She turned to look at Brad. "Aren't you going to tell me what it is now?"

"Patience, my dear, patience," he joked. "I want

to see the look on your face when you find out. We'll be around the front in a minute." His arm slipped gently around her shoulders as he guided her toward the front of the theater.

The big red letters of the theater marquee suddenly loomed large in front of them. "Well, what do you think?" Brad said triumphantly. "Aren't you surprised?"

Surprised wasn't quite the word for what Laura felt. Sick was more like it. She'd had no idea that there was a special one-night Woody Allen festival in town that night. He had been Michael's and her favorite; they'd seen some of his movies four and five times together. Laura tried hard to keep her composure until they were seated in the darkened theater, and she hoped that the disappointment she'd noticed on Brad's face was only her imagination. Laura thought to herself, It's as if Michael's just supposed to be here. Confusion flooded her heart and her mind. How can I miss Michael so much and still want to be with Brad? What's the matter with me? she wondered.

Laura could almost sense Brad's eyes searching her face from time to time, but he never said anything. When the lights went up, they walked from the theater silently. Finally, Brad looked at Laura, his eyes clouded with sadness. "Sorry," he said, "I guess Debbie gave me kind of a bum steer. She told me that you're a big Woody Allen fan, so when I saw something about this festival in the paper, I just figured that I'd surprise you. I'll know not to do that again. Actually, I'm not that big a fan of his myself, anyway."

Laura didn't say anything. How could she explain to Brad that she loved Woody Allen but that that was a part of herself and her life that belonged to Michael? What was wrong with her? She knew she had to live in the present. But suddenly she couldn't let go of the past. Confusion swirling inside her, Laura said only, "How about coming back to my house? I'll make you one of those great hot fudge sundaes that you like so much at the hospital soda fountain."

"Okay," said Brad. "Sounds pretty good." In no time, they were headed for Laura's house. Pulling up to the curb across from the long, winding walkway that led to her front door, Brad turned off the motor and shut off his car lights. Laura could feel the warmth of his body as he put his arms around her. He leaned down to kiss her, but almost involuntarily, she pulled back. Brad turned away from her as if he'd been burned and then slammed his hand against the steering wheel.

"Laura, I'm really tired of having to compete with another guy whenever we're together. You and I have a lot in common. We could have a great time together. And I'm not afraid to compete against any other guy for you. But I can't compete with a ghost, and I won't even try anymore!"

To her complete horror, Laura realized that big tears had begun to run down her cheeks. When she tried to look at Brad to speak to him, she could only see his face through a mist. "I—I'm sorry, Brad. I really do like being with you. It's just—it's just—" Suddenly, the whole thing seemed too overwhelming to explain, especially when she didn't really understand it herself.

Brad had calmed down considerably. His voice was no longer angry, just dully resigned, as he said, "I guess I should have known. The guys tried to warn me. They told me all about Michael and how hard all of them had taken his death. They told me that you had been his girl and that ever since he'd died, you'd never dated anyone else." Brad sighed and continued talking almost as if he were trying to straighten things out in his own mind. "I thought the reason was because those guys were his friends and none of them wanted to be the one to be the first to take you out. But I didn't know Michael. I mean, I'm really sorry about what happened, but it was almost two years ago, and when I met you, I thought you were pretty special." Brad looked helplessly at Laura. "Listen, why don't I walk you up to your door?"

Unable to speak, Laura merely nodded. They walked to the door, and the only sound was the clicking of their shoes against the sidewalk. When they reached Laura's front door, Brad bent down and brushed his lips against Laura's forehead. "You're a terrific girl. But I won't bother you anymore, because I don't want to be the thing that's making you so unhappy. But, Laura, I promise you this—" There was a strange huskiness in Brad's voice. "If Michael was really as special as he sounds, he wouldn't want to make you this unhappy, either."

With that, Brad turned and walked quickly to his car. Laura stood frozen on her doorstep, watching the Saab roar away and turn rapidly around a corner.

Chapter 13

OⴲO

O*n Monday morning, Laura realized with a jolt* that she'd completely forgotten about Paula. She'd meant to call her on Sunday to make sure that everything was going okay, but she'd been too caught up in her problems with Brad to remember. She was still dreading chemistry class because she'd have to see Brad, and she didn't know if she had the strength to face him. Walking down the hallway, lost in her own thoughts, Laura saw Paula out of the corner of her eye. "Paula," she called, "how is everything?"

Paula looked unconcerned. "Everything's just fine. I told you it would be."

Paula's cheery manner gave Laura an uneasy feeling. "Paula, you aren't going to try anything to get back at Miss McVinnis, are you?"

Paula laughed. "Of course not. I think you're

right; the woman has no heart. I'm not even sure she's human, so why bother with her? It's a waste of time." Laura raised an eyebrow, thinking that that wasn't exactly the way she'd described Miss McVinnis. The woman was really a good teacher, and she explained things well and was always available for extra help. The problem was, she just didn't allow any bending of the rules in her class—even when it was for a very good reason. "Besides," Paula continued, "I have a feeling that Miss McVinnis will get what's coming to her soon enough."

"But, Paula, if you didn't talk to Miss McVinnis, what did you do to solve your problems?" Laura persisted. For a minute, she felt a little guilty; after all, if Paula had taken care of everything, then Laura was just being nosy. She quickly added, "You don't have to tell me if you don't want to."

Paula shrugged. "I just told my mother that since she and Dad got divorced, I haven't been able to concentrate very well. I gave her this whole big story about how tough these last few months have been." Paula smiled slightly. "Mom said how glad she was that I had finally opened up to her and that maybe part of my trouble was that she'd been expecting too much of me. Can you believe it? Anyway, I convinced her that I didn't really need chemistry in the first place. And Miss Johnson is going to let me be a teacher's assistant for her instead, so I can make up the credit. So you see, I'll have lots more time to plan the pledge-initiation prank, and you poor things will still have to suffer through chemistry." Paula patted Laura on the shoulder. "Thanks, though. You were sweet to try to help me out."

Paula went off to talk to one of the pledges, and Laura was left standing in the hall with an amazed look on her face. Once again, Paula had found a way around a crisis in her life. Thank goodness she hadn't tried to argue with Miss McVinnis to do it.

The day dragged on slowly until the bell rang for chemistry class. Laura went to the rest room until the last possible minute so that she could slip into her seat without having to talk to Brad. And in spite of her efforts not to look at him, their eyes locked once during class. Laura was shocked by the hurt look in Brad's eyes. How can life be so confusing? she wondered. How can I make myself stop remembering Michael? When the class ended, Brad hurried out of chemistry before Laura even had a chance to gather her books together.

After school, Laura decided to go home and talk things over with her mother. This was simply too big a problem for her to solve by herself. But when she got home, no one was there. On the kitchen table, there was a note from her mother saying that she was at a Kenilworth Junior League meeting and that she'd left some freshly baked cookies in the cookie jar. She'd added that she wouldn't be home until seven and that her father would be working late. Laura read the note a second time. She'd have to wait to talk to her mother. She knew that it was only a few more hours, but inside she was ready to explode. Laura thought about calling Ellen or Debbie—maybe they could help her. She sat with the telephone receiver in her hand and even dialed the first five digits of Ellen's number before hanging up the phone.

That won't work, she told herself with a sad sigh. None of her friends could truly understand what she was going through. And she hoped they would never have to experience the terrible pain or the lingering loyalty she was feeling now. Laura knew that she'd just have to wait for her mother to come home. And, honestly, Laura wasn't even sure that her mother could do anything.

Pacing the house, Laura was brimming with nervous energy. She couldn't sit still long enough to do her homework, and she couldn't relax enough to watch TV. Grabbing her jacket and purse, she decided to go over to the hospital. Maybe working would help.

A few minutes later, Laura was pulling her car into the parking lot at Kenilworth Memorial. She stopped at the volunteer desk to report in and JoAnn said, "The kids here are so excited about the play that you're doing. Apparently one little boy was even scheduled to go home today, but he begged the doctor to let him stay until the weekend so he could see the play!" JoAnn chuckled. "Can you believe that—a kid volunteering to stay in the hospital?"

Laura smiled. "JoAnn, I wish I could say that the play was my idea. But to tell you the truth,

this is the first time I've even heard there was
one. Who's coordinating it? Are you sure it was
one of the Pearls?"

JoAnn punched something into the computer.
"Gee, Laura, I just assumed that the play was
your idea. I mean, you've organized just about
everything else that the Pearls have done this
year. Hang on and I'll find out who it was." She
read the printed words that came on the screen.
"Molly Gold—play scheduled for Saturday morning." JoAnn punched another button. "She's here
now, working in the snack bar, if you want to talk
to her."

"Thanks, JoAnn. I'll be back for an assignment
in just a minute." Laura headed quickly for the
hospital snack bar. She found Molly standing behind the soda fountain, making a milk shake.

Molly waved and smiled. After handing the
man beside the counter his milk shake, she turned
to look at Laura. "Hi." Glancing around a little
self-consciously, she added, "I guess you could
say that I decided to find the sweetest job in the
hospital."

Laura laughed. "Don't knock it. The hospital
needs all of the volunteer help it can get. And
since they don't pay us, there's more money left
for things that really help the patients." Laura
suddenly remembered why she'd wanted to talk
to Molly. "Hey, I heard you're putting on a play
for the kids. JoAnn even said that they're so excited that the hospital is having trouble getting

some of them to check out even if they've gotten well."

Molly looked embarrassed. "Oh, she's exaggerating. It's really no big deal. We finished a fairy-tale characterization project in theater class, and I just told some of the students that it might be fun to perform their act for a real audience. They're all such a bunch of hams that they jumped at the chance."

Laura felt a rush of warmth for the younger girl. She knew how hard it was to get kids to give up a Saturday morning to spend at the hospital, so she knew that Molly must have been very convincing. "I think it's great," she said enthusiastically.

Molly shrugged. "Well, I'm glad you think so; I don't think Paula was too pleased. She said that working here was a Pearl privilege and not just anyone should come tromping in."

Laura tried to reassure Molly that she'd done the right thing, but the pledge waved her off. "Listen, it's okay. I can't seem to get along well with Paula, and that's that. I don't like it, but since I'm the pledge, I have to learn to give in whenever we disagree." Suddenly, Molly stopped, and a deep blush covered her face. "I'm sorry. I realize that the Pearls are all sisters, and I look forward to one day being one of them. I shouldn't have said what I did."

Laura was torn between reassuring Molly that Paula could indeed be difficult and defending Paula because she knew she should. Before Laura could say anything, however, Molly was called away to wait on a customer. Returning quickly, Molly said, "Listen, I'm really sorry I said anything about Paula. I guess that every Pearl feels a pretty strong loyalty to the group. Besides, even if we don't always agree, once the pledge class all decides on something, we have to follow through. Otherwise, how can we have any real unity, right?" Laura got the sense that Molly's casual words were more of a question than a statement. She didn't know what she could say to help. So, after a few more minutes, Laura returned to the volunteer center to get her job assignment for the afternoon.

By the time the afternoon was over and Laura had driven home, she was feeling much better about things. Somehow, she thought, pulling into her driveway, your own problems never seem as great when you see what other people have had to overcome. But as she walked into the house, she decided that she still wanted to talk things over with her mother.

Waiting until dinner was finished, she casually asked her mother if she had anything important to do that evening. Laura noticed a concerned look pass between her parents. Her mother said, "No, I'm not doing anything important. I promised to make some cakes for the Junior League bake sale, but I'd love some company."

Somehow, knowing that her mother wasn't just sitting there staring at her made talking to her easier. But it still wasn't going to be easy. "Mom, remember how we talked after Michael died and you were so worried that I'd withdraw from everything? And I promised you I wouldn't, and I didn't, right?"

"Yes," said Mrs. Clark. "Dad and I knew how hard it was for you, and we were proud of you for trying so hard."

Laura looked toward the floor. "Well, I don't think you'd be so proud now." The words tumbled out in a rush as she explained her problem. "I've really hurt Brad. I know it. And the awful thing is, I don't want to hurt anyone, especially not him. He's such a great guy, and so much fun to be with. But all of a sudden I feel Michael's presence so strongly. Mom, I miss him so much. I feel even worse than I did right after he—well, right after it first happened."

Mrs. Clark's brow wrinkled with worry. "And you don't understand what's happening, right?"

Laura's voice was shaky. "I think I'm going crazy. I want to be with Brad; I think about him, I look forward to seeing him, and then when we're together, I wish that I'd just stayed home."

Mrs. Clark laid a gentle hand on Laura's shoulder. "Honey, that's not so strange. You've gone out a lot since Michael died. You've been with lots of friends. But this is the first boy that you've cared about since Michael. You probably feel disloyal to his memory." Laura nodded. "That's perfectly natural. But you can't live in the past; Michael wouldn't have wanted that, and I think you know that. Laura, you'll never be able to replace

Michael—to recapture exactly what you two had—but that doesn't mean there can't be other very special people in your life, too."

"Mom, I think I love Brad." It was the first time Laura had allowed herself to fully admit it. "But it's too late. I've already ruined everything."

Mrs. Clark pretended to be busy with her baking. "Laura dear, you can't know that unless you talk to Brad."

"But, Mom, I can't do that. It would just be too—too— I'm not good at that kind of thing," she finished lamely.

Chapter 14

~○━○~

For two days, Laura thought about what her mother had said. But every time she thought she could walk up to Brad and tell him she needed to talk to him, she faltered. He occupied almost all of her thoughts. Then, on Thursday, Laura heard some news that took her mind off her own problems. By lunchtime, everyone knew that old Miss McVinnis had actually missed a day of school. The news, had it been about any other teacher, would have hardly raised a yawn. But Miss McVinnis had been around so long that even Mr. Madden had had her as a teacher. As far as anyone knew, she hadn't missed a day of school—ever!

Today, however, all that had changed. And in chemistry the poor substitute never had a chance. The kids went wild at having a day of complete freedom. Everyone wondered why Miss McVinnis had finally missed a day of school. But Laura's mind was still half preoccupied with thoughts of Brad, and she barely listened to the most outrageous ideas people had come up with to explain her absence.

After school that afternoon, Laura decided to take a long walk and see if she could plan out exactly what she'd say to Brad. Maybe if she had the exact words in her mind she could manage to get them out. If she couldn't tell Brad in person, maybe she could at least write them in a letter to him. But the farther away she got from school, the less her thoughts seemed to make sense. She phrased and rephrased her words, paying little attention to how long or where she had been walking. Finally, she looked up, rather amazed to find that she was a fair distance from school. Suddenly, more aware of her surroundings, she noticed the cute, gingerbread-style houses around her. They were much smaller than the ones in her own neighborhood, but they had a charm all their own. In the distance, Laura saw a woman moving in her direction. The sun was in her eyes, and she couldn't make out who it might be until she was almost upon her. Even then, Laura barely recognized the woman. "Miss McVinnis!" The words popped out of Laura's mouth before she had a chance to think. The normally precise teacher looked totally unglued. Her white hair was sticking out of her bun every which way. The glasses she wore didn't cover the frantic look on her face. The lady in front of Laura looked nothing like the formidable Miss McVinnis in chemistry class; instead, she resembled a wounded old woman who'd lost faith in life.

For a moment, the teacher seemed as stunned to see Laura as Laura had been to see her. Then a ray of intense hope passed across the woman's face. "You've found her," she half whispered. "That's why you're here. Oh, bless you. I knew she couldn't be gone forever. Where is she?"

"Miss McVinnis—" Laura could feel her own eyes welling with tears as she felt the teacher's pain. Even so, she had no idea what her teacher was talking about. "I'm sorry—I, uh, I haven't found anyone. But I'll help you look. We could call the police; maybe they could search. Who's missing?"

The teacher seemed to shrink before her eyes. "Then you haven't found her. My poor Scooter is gone forever. I just know it. But I won't give up. I can't give up. I know she wouldn't have just wandered away."

Laura tried again. "Scooter—is that your dog?"

Miss McVinnis shook her head. "Much more than just a dog; she's my companion, my friend. She's only a miniature schnauzer, but to me she's everything. Oh, what could have happened to her? I've been looking everywhere since last night."

Not knowing what to say but wanting to make the teacher feel better, Laura lied. "We all really missed you at school today."

But the teacher didn't even seem to hear her. "She's gray and white, and she's always come as soon as I call her name. She can't be gone; she just can't. Why would someone take my Scooter?" Without waiting for an answer, the teacher continued down the street, calling the dog's name into the wind.

Laura stood where she was. Her mouth fell open as she tried to make her mind believe that this poor old woman was the same controlled drillmaster who ran their chemistry class. Laura knew that some of her friends would have thought the situation was funny. But Laura recognized that as strange as it seemed, Miss McVinnis's pain was absolutely real. Scooter was as important to her as a person might be. Laura knew all too well how that felt, and she tried to think what she could do to help find the dog.

"Here, Scooter," she called as she began retracing her own steps. But as much as she wanted it to happen, no dog appeared. It was strange; she'd never even thought that Miss McVinnis might have a life outside the chemistry room before. Suddenly, Laura wondered to herself what Paula would think of the woman she'd called a robot if she could see her now. Then Laura began to get an uneasy feeling in her stomach. What had Paula said about Miss McVinnis? She searched her memory for the exact words—something about how the teacher would get hers. Oh, it's just a coincidence, Laura reassured herself. Just a silly coincidence. But she walked a little faster, anyway.

Reaching the school parking lot, Laura got in her car and drove straight to Paula's. Once she arrived and saw the surprised look on Paula's delicate face, Laura felt ridiculous. She couldn't just accuse her sorority sister of stealing their chemistry teacher's dog. Laura took a deep breath. "Paula, I really need to know about the pledge prank. Has it started? What are the girls doing?"

Paula's perfect smile disappeared. "Laura, did Susie put you up to this? Because if she did, you tell her for me that it didn't work. You know that the pledge prank is supposed to be kept a secret until after it's over. And the pledges have worked really hard on this. Why spoil it?"

Laura tried again. "Paula, I need to know. It's really important." Paula wouldn't budge. "Okay, at least tell me this—does it involve Miss McVinnis?"

There was a hard look in Paula's eyes. "Laura, the girls voted to keep it a secret, remember? And, anyway, it will be over soon enough, and then all of the Pearls will know."

Laura tried again, but Paula was firm. Laura hated confrontation, and she'd just about convinced herself that she should just forget about Paula and leave when a picture of a grief-stricken Miss McVinnis flashed once again in front of her. "Paula, just tell me on your Pearl honor that the prank has nothing to do with Miss McVinnis and I'll go."

Paula appeared to be weighing her odds. "Laura, it's silly to stand out here talking on the doorstep. I don't know where my manners are. Why don't you come on in?" Laura followed her sorority sister inside the house. "Do you want something to drink or a snack or something?" Paula asked, suddenly the gracious hostess.

Laura refused, saying that she could only stay a minute. Paula switched tactics. "You know, Laura, I think I've figured this whole thing out. Molly Gold came to you, didn't she?" Paula looked very much like a wronged friend. "I've tried so hard to keep some amount of unity among the girls, but I guess that wasn't enough. Just because Molly and a few of her friends didn't like the prank, they couldn't stand not letting it out of the bag. Frankly, I'm disappointed in you. The prank was passed by a majority of the pledges. When Molly came whining to you, I really think you had an obligation to back me up about pledge unity."

This was all moving so quickly. Laura tried to straighten things out. "Molly didn't tell me anything. It's just that I saw Miss McVinnis today. You wouldn't have believed it was her." Laura attempted to tell Paula how distraught the woman had been, but Paula didn't seem to care.

"Laura, I think you're getting a little hysterical. No one poisoned the dog; the pledges are going to return it safe and sound. We've just borrowed it for a couple of days. And, believe me, the girls are taking very good care of it. It was all just done in fun."

"But Miss McVinnis—"

Paula interrupted Laura. "She not only threw one of your sorority sisters out of class and failed her for the semester but also humiliated her in front of the entire school. This is the lady you're so worried about? Laura, let me tell you two things: first of all, what we're doing to her is not nearly as bad as what she did to me, and second of all, I'm your sorority sister. What is she to you except tons of hard homework?"

In the end, Laura caved in. Hating herself, she let Paula talk her into leaving. It was not only that Laura hated confrontation, but Paula had made Laura doubt herself. Maybe she was being overly sensitive, she thought. Maybe Miss McVinnis shouldn't have been so hard on Paula. Those reasons got her almost three blocks from Paula's when Laura's conscience made her turn around.

Clenching her fingernails into her palms, she made up her mind that she would not be swayed this time. She rang the doorbell, and Paula answered. Laura took a deep breath. "Paula, we need to talk."

Chapter 15

*L*aura stood her ground. "There is an old lady out there who is half hysterical because she is afraid that the thing she loves the most in the world is hurt or dead. And we're responsible for that. Pranks are supposed to be funny, and maybe this one started out that way, but it isn't funny now. You have to return that dog. Now!"

Paula's calm smile didn't falter; if anything, her voice got even sweeter and friendlier. "Now, Laura, I thought we just settled all this. Look, if it will make you feel better, the dog will be back safe and sound on Saturday."

But Laura was no longer listening to Paula's persuasive words. Instead, she was frantic. What difference did all her work in the hospital make if now she had the chance to really help someone, she didn't? Suddenly, Laura realized that no amount of reasoning was going to change Paula's mind. "Look, Paula," she finally said, "I don't want to do this; I really don't. But I don't have a choice. If you won't return the dog tonight, I'm going to go tell Miss McVinnis that Scooter is safe and that we took her."

Paula's eyes narrowed. "You don't want to do that, Laura. Think about it. You can go to Miss McVinnis if you want; but think about what'll happen from there. Will she take the whole thing as the joke it was supposed to be? Will she see that no harm was done? Oh, no, Miss McVinnis's thanks to you will be to report us to Mrs. O'Neill, who will get rid of Pearl forever. Is that really the way you want to be remembered, Laura? As the girl who ended the Pearl sorority after eighty-seven years of leadership at Taft High?" Seeing the anxiety creep into Laura's eyes, she continued. "My pledges have planned this prank. They've worked hard to pull it off, and I'm not going to stop the whole plan so you can make that old witch happy." Paula looked absolutely confident.

Laura shifted her weight from one foot to the other while a tense silence hung in the air. She knew that Paula was right—Miss McVinnis would play by the rules. She would report the girls, and according to school policy, the group would be banned from school events for a year. That would effectively mean the end of Pearl. That didn't just mean that Paula would be punished, but Debbie and Ellen and Susie and everyone else. "I—I have to think," Laura said. But her heart cried out,

Why can't you just see how stupid this whole thing is? Why does it have to divide us? But it was too late for that now. They had already been divided.

Laura got in her car and began to drive. She wasn't even sure where she was going; she just hoped it would clear her mind. Was she really risking the future of the entire sorority because she was overly sensitive? Did it really matter if Miss McVinnis was upset for one more day? Hadn't pledge pranks been going on for years?

Laura continued to drive, but then she got an idea. She turned and headed for Molly Gold's house. She got out of the car and rang the bell. Molly was surprised to see Laura but welcomed her into her house nevertheless. "I can't stay," Laura said. "I just have to ask you a question. I know I'm putting you on the spot, but you've got to answer me."

Molly looked worried. "Laura, what's wrong? Of course I'll help if I can."

"I know about the pledge prank. I just want to know one thing. Why did you decide to do it?"

Molly turned white as a sheet. "I can't believe you found out. That's terrible. I mean, we went through all that, and now we won't get to go active."

"What are you talking about?" Laura asked.

"Paula said that if any active found out about the prank before it was over, we'd have to stay pledges for another month."

Laura sighed and shook her head. "Why did you decide on that prank?"

Molly looked uncomfortable, as if she were further betraying her pledge sisters, but remembering the way Laura had helped her the night she'd confided in Laura at the hospital, she said, "I'm telling you because I know you'd never ask if it wasn't important. But, please, don't tell anyone I told you. Come on back to my room; this will take a few minutes."

The two girls sat down on the thick, plush lavender carpet in Molly's room, and, taking a deep breath, Molly began her story. She spoke rapidly. "We had about thirty different prank ideas, but none of them seemed good enough. Either they'd been done before, or they were impossible to pull off. We were afraid we'd never get to go active. Then Paula came to the last pledge meeting and told us that our worries were over. Then she announced that she'd figured out the perfect prank. She told us about Miss McVinnis's dog and said we needed to do it right away. Some of the girls seemed to love the idea, but others—including me—didn't like it. We argued that it seemed mean; I was worried that something might happen to the dog while we had it. But Paula was really persuasive. Of course, none of us have Miss McVinnis in class, because she only teaches upperclassmen, but we've heard stories about her. And Paula told us lots more terrible things. She said that Miss McVinnis had tried to humiliate the sorority and that the actives would be really proud of us for getting back at her."

Laura winced, thinking to herself that Paula's humiliation by Miss McVinnis had nothing to do with her being a Pearl. "Go ahead," she said. "What happened then?"

"Well," Molly continued, "Paula said that the whole school would be really proud of us because Miss McVinnis had made so many kids squirm that they would love to see someone make her squirm. We said we were afraid that the dog might get sick while we had it. I mean, what if it died? But Paula said that we could certainly take care of a dog for a few days without anything happening to him. Finally, she said that she'd already figured out exactly how we could kidnap him and that if we did it this week, it wouldn't be too much longer until we went active."

Molly sighed and pushed some strands of her long brown hair behind her ears. "At first, I argued against the plan. And some of the other pledges agreed with me. If we'd voted right then, I don't know if it would have passed. But instead, Lynnell Johnson—who thinks just like Paula—told everyone that she thought taking Miss McVinnis's dog was the best idea ever and that anyone who wasn't in favor of it should present something better or be quiet. Obviously, the vote came out for Paula's prank idea. We all agreed that it had won fair and square and that we'd stay unified as a pledge class and pull it off."

Molly's Persian white cat had jumped up on her

lap, and she was stroking it absently as she talked. "After all my problems with Paula, I just didn't think I should be the one to try to stop the prank after it had been voted on. Still, I haven't enjoyed doing it; I just keep thinking of how I would feel if someone took my cat even for a day. I'd feel just horrible." Molly looked ashamed. "I went along with the prank because I didn't have the courage to stop it."

Laura suddenly felt at peace with herself. She thanked Molly and got up to leave. "What are you going to do?" Molly asked. "Why did you want to know about all this?"

Laura smiled. "It's probably better if I don't tell you. But thanks; you've helped me a lot."

Five minutes later, Laura eased her car into Paula's driveway for the third time that afternoon. The sun was setting, and Laura realized that it must be almost dinnertime. She rang the bell, and Paula answered the door immediately. "Don't tell me." Paula smiled sweetly. "You've come back to say that you're sorry for being so worried about the prank. Well, don't apologize. We all love you for worrying; we just have to make sure it doesn't get out of hand."

Laura looked at Paula, and in a voice that sounded much firmer than her own, she said, "No, Paula. I've come to tell you that the prank must end right now. Don't you see—if this prank isn't stopped now, the next one might be a little more dangerous or a little meaner. And everyone would rationalize that no one wanted to be the one to be a wet blanket. You may not understand this, but it's not just for Miss McVinnis that this prank has to be stopped; it's for all of us. It's for the future of Pearl, and even if we do get kicked off campus, that will be better than sitting back and doing nothing and knowing someday that someone was really hurt because no one would stand up and stop it now."

Paula stared back at Laura carefully. "Brava, Laura. Well said." Paula gave a little clap. But she also knew instinctively that this time quiet, sensitive Laura was not going to give in. She really was going to tell Miss McVinnis. "Okay, Laura, if you feel that strongly about it, we'll give the dog back to her tonight. So you can quit worrying. But I want you to realize that I'm doing this for you because I'm worried about your feelings; I couldn't care less about Miss McVinnis."

Laura looked doubtful. "Paula, I know the prank was your idea. You should be the one to return the dog, not some pledge. If you want, I'll even come with you. It won't be so bad; really it won't."

Paula sighed. She just wanted to get the whole thing over with. "Okay, okay, I'll do it. But only on one condition: no one ever finds out about this. I'll sneak the dog back to the old witch, but the story will have to be that it got lost and found its way home. The pledges and I will plan another prank, and none of the Pearls will ever know that this one failed."

Laura thought for a moment. All she really wanted was to get the dog back to Miss McVinnis tonight. She didn't want the woman to worry any longer. And now Paula had agreed to do just that. "There's just one thing that bothers me," Laura said. "How will you get the dog back to Miss McVinnis safely without actually giving it to her?"

Paula's voice took on a hard edge. "Oh, for heaven's sake, Laura. I'll let the dog out on her street, and I'm sure it will run home and bark at the door. Now, leave me alone."

Laura felt a hundred years old. "It won't do, Paula. The dog could get hit by a car, or someone else could take it. We've got to make sure it gets home."

Paula's mind was working a mile a minute, for she was smart enough to know that there was no use in arguing with Laura now. Her heart-shaped lips pouted. "Laura, I'm really disappointed in you. I mean, I thought we were friends. But obviously I was wrong. Okay, I'll get the dumb dog, and I'll dump it in Miss McVinnis's fenced-in back-yard. But I'm only doing it your way because I know that if I don't, you'll go and tattle on everyone. But let me tell you one thing: I'd better not get caught, because if I do, I'll be kicked out of school, and so will the Pearl sorority. And if that happens, just remember that it will be all your fault."

Chapter 16

○●○

*L*aura *walked slowly back to her car. Well, she* told herself, it's done. Getting in the car, she put the key in the ignition, started the motor, and then turned it off again. A few minutes later, Paula came out of the house with her own car keys.

"What are you doing? Waiting to see if I've kept my word?" Paula asked her in a tense, angry voice. "Is this the trusting Laura that the Pearls all know and love?"

"No," said Laura slowly. "It's just that this was my idea, and if we get caught, we'll get caught together. I know you don't believe me right now, but I am your friend. And I don't want you to get in trouble. I just wish this whole prank had never happened."

"You are about the last person in the world I

feel like being with right now." Paula stormed off and headed for her own car. Before she got there, she turned around and called over her shoulder. "Just go away. I'll take care of this without any more of your *help*."

Laura watched Paula's blue Honda roar away. Then she started her own car and headed home, wondering if anything would ever be the same again for the girls in Pearl. *I did it for all of us,* she tried to reassure herself as she drove, and seeing the picture of the terror-stricken teacher in her mind, she knew that there was nothing else she could have done.

Still, the whole incident had left her with no appetite. She told her mother at dinner that she wasn't feeling well and went to her room. *Tomorrow this will all be over,* she told herself. *Tomorrow everything will be okay again.* She flopped down on her bed and fell asleep.

Awakening with a start, Laura saw her mother bending over her. "Laura, I hate to wake you," said Mrs. Clark, "but Paula's in the other room. She seems terribly upset, and she says she must talk to you."

"It's okay, Mom. Could you please tell her to come back to my room?" Laura said with a growing sense of dread.

Moments later, Paula walked in and shut the door behind herself. "Paula?" Laura started to ask. But before she could say anything else, Paula began to cry, and soon her body was heaving with sobs. Many agonizing minutes went by before Paula had calmed down enough to speak.

"It was so awful," Paula whispered. "I was just getting ready to drop the dog over the fence when this light was flashed in my eyes. It was Miss McVinnis. Molly, Lynnell, and I just froze."

"Molly? Lynnell?" Laura asked, feeling confused. "What were they doing there?"

At this point, Paula figured there was no point in hiding anything. "I told them we were ending the pledge prank early. Since two other girls had taken the dog, I said they were the pledges I'd chosen to return it." Paula's voice was flat and dull. "I figured that that way I'd get you off my back and still make the pledges think we'd pulled a successful prank—and I'd still be able to beat Susie for president. But none of that matters now. You see, Miss McVinnis told us that she was reporting all three of us to the principal tomorrow and was going to recommend that we all be suspended for the rest of the semester. She also said that she was sure Mrs. O'Neill would have further disciplinary action for the sorority itself."

Chapter 17

O=O

*L*aura didn't know what she thought she was going to accomplish, but she knew she at least had to try. She'd never been so scared in her life. What if Miss McVinnis ended up kicking her out of school, too? She rang the teacher's doorbell, still unsure of what she was going to say. Miss McVinnis answered, and while she looked very tired, the frantic expression had already disappeared from her face.

"I, uh, I'm glad you got your dog back safely," Laura stuttered.

"Thank you, Laura, but I'm really quite tired and not much in the mood for company. Perhaps you could see me after class tomorrow if you need something."

Laura could not believe her own boldness. "I'm sorry, Miss McVinnis, but I can't wait until then.

I'll only take a few minutes of your time, *please*."
There was a note of desperation in her voice.

The teacher motioned her in, and once she was
there, Laura suddenly felt tongue-tied. She began
trying to explain, but nothing was coming out
right. Finally, she sighed. "Miss McVinnis, I know
it was terrible to take your dog. It never should
have been done, and nothing can make up for the
fear you felt when Scooter was gone. But the girls
who took him—and everyone in Pearl—well, we've
all learned an important lesson, and that's why
we brought him back tonight."

The teacher's tone was forbidding. "Are you
saying, Laura Clark, that I should simply thank
these young hooligans for returning my dog after
they stole it and be happy that they learned
something?"

"No, ma'am, I'm not."

"Then perhaps you should tell me exactly what
you do want."

Laura ran a nervous hand through her short,
dark curls and began again. She tried to explain
that the prank had been done out of thoughtless-
ness rather than cruelty and that the girls had
taken good care of the dog. They'd never intended to hurt it in any way. She tried to explain
that suspending all of the Pearls would only make
matters worse, and finally, she tried to explain
about Pearl. "I know you probably think sorori-
ties are terrible right now and that pledge pranks
are stupid, but Pearl is a lot of good things, too."
She talked about its service work at the hospital;

she talked about the friendships that endured even after Pearls had grown, married, and moved to different parts of the country.

Miss McVinnis listened without comment. Scooter was sleeping quietly at her feet. Finally, Laura stopped. It was the longest, most impassioned speech she'd ever given in her life. And yet she had no idea if it had helped even the smallest bit. The two of them sat in silence for a minute, and then the teacher said, "Laura, what exactly do you propose I do?"

Laura had no idea what to say. She hadn't thought about what an appropriate punishment would be. "I don't know," she said. "All I could think about was getting Scooter back to you right away so you wouldn't worry. I can't tell you what to do; I just wanted you to understand the whole situation."

The teacher looked sad, and she spoke more to herself than to Laura. "I don't think you can begin to imagine what I went through during the time that Scooter was missing." Her tone grew stern, as if she'd once again realized Laura's presence. "So you have come to me tonight without any proposed solution?"

"I guess not," Laura said, feeling defeated. She looked squarely at her teacher. "Miss McVinnis, your class has been hard; you've been demanding, but you've always been fair. I just wanted you to have all the facts so you could be fair now, too."

The teacher stood. "Very well, you've had your

say." There was the vaguest twinkle in her eyes. "And I daresay that took some courage. Now, if you don't mind, I've had quite enough commotion and company for one night."

Laura left, unsure whether her visit had done any good at all.

Chapter 18

○•○

*O*n *Friday morning, Miss McVinnis sent for Laura* after first hour. "I want to see all the members of Pearl in my classroom after school today. Can you arrange for that?"

"I—I think so," Laura said.

"Very well. I'll deal with you all then."

Getting messages to all the actives and pledges wasn't easy. When they were notified, some girls were immediately scared. Others, still unaware of what had happened, were merely perplexed when they were told to be in Miss McVinnis's classroom immediately after last hour. A few people had argued that they had other plans and had been told that the future of the sorority depended on their being there.

At five minutes past three, Miss McVinnis's chemistry classroom was filled from one end to the other with members of Pearl—both pledges and actives. Every seat was taken, and some girls were standing against the wall. Miss McVinnis cleared her throat and began to speak. "I always tell my chemistry students that we cannot figure out an unknown until we first establish that which is known. That is what I am going to do right now. The Pearl pledges, advised by their pledge trainer, Paula Parker, stole my dog. That makes them thieves. They returned the dog safely, but that makes their initial act no less terrible, nor does it compensate for the great anguish I suffered. Imagine someone taking the thing that was nearest and dearest to you and you'll know how I felt. So their deed cannot, and will not, go unpunished. One of your members, however, has explained to me that there are some other factors to be considered here and that she feels that a valuable lesson has already been learned." Miss McVinnis adjusted her glasses on her nose and nodded to Mrs. O'Neill.

Mrs. O'Neill came forward. "I don't have to tell you girls how disappointed I am in you. I thought I could count on the Pearls to set a good example on this campus, and frankly I wouldn't have blamed Miss McVinnis if she'd wanted to follow the letter of the law and ban all Pearl activities from this campus for a year." The girls all gasped at once. "However, she has agreed instead to punish the sorority by asking them to spend two full Saturdays this month cleaning graffiti from the gym bleachers. Is there anyone here who objects to that?"

The chemistry teacher added smugly, "Perhaps this will help you develop some group unity."

Mrs. O'Neill wound the meeting up by saying, "Girls, I know you probably aren't very happy now, but you should be very grateful that you were caught. In spite of my lectures against it, I feel that pledge pranks have gotten out of hand and this sort of thing needs to be stopped before somebody is really hurt."

The girls fidgeted in their seats. The sorority had been formed in the spirit of fun and friendship, and everyone felt terrible that things had gotten so out of hand. "Miss Parker," the chemistry teacher said dryly, "I'd like to speak with you. The rest of you girls are dismissed."

The Pearls walked out silently, but within a couple of minutes the hallways were filled with conversations. "I am never again," said Molly to another pledge, "going to let myself be talked into doing something I know is wrong in the first place."

Laura headed for her locker, feeling only slightly victorious. Miss McVinnis had gotten her dog back safely, the Pearls weren't going to be kicked off campus, and the lesson about pledge pranks was one she didn't think the Pearls would ever forget. They wouldn't stop planning initiation pranks— and she wouldn't want them to—but maybe they wouldn't be so mean next time. As for Paula, Laura had a feeling that her meeting with Miss

McVinnis would be interesting, but she was fairly certain that the teacher wouldn't do anything more than reprimand her sorority sister. Actually, underneath her gruff exterior, Miss McVinnis had turned out to be a pretty nice person.

Laura walked to the parking lot, thinking of her mother's often-repeated statement: "The harder it is to do something, the more important it probably is to do it." Laura knew how true this was. She just hoped that eventually Paula would see that, too.

As Laura made her way to the parking lot, several of the Pearls called to her that they were heading to Le Finis to talk things over. They asked Laura to join them, but Laura didn't want to. She'd talked enough. Arriving at home, she put her books on the desk and flopped on her bed. I wonder, she thought. If Michael were here, what would he have thought of all this? She began to wonder for the first time if they would still be going together if Michael had lived. He would be off in college somewhere, she reminded herself. And I'm so different in so many ways from the way I was then. Suddenly, Laura knew what she had to do just as surely as she'd known what to do about Paula. She sat up on her bed. "I can't live in the past. I told myself that I wasn't doing that, but I was. I went to parties and dances and even occasionally joined other couples. But in the back of my mind I knew that by going places alone, I was reminding everyone that Michael should have been there." Tears filled Laura's big brown eyes. "I can't carry you around with me everywhere I go anymore, Michael," Laura said to an empty room. "If I do, I can't really live or grow myself. But, Michael, I swear I'll never forget you. There will always be a special place in my heart that is reserved just for you."

Laura was so tired that she slept through dinner on Friday night and late into Saturday morning. She was awakened by the phone ringing. "Hi," came Susie's cheery voice. "I thought you might like to know what happened to Paula. How's this for ironic? Paula 'volunteered' to spend every afternoon for the rest of the semester cleaning up the chemistry labs for Miss McVinnis." Then Susie laughed. "I'll bet that before the semester is over, she'll manage to convince everyone that she's doing it just to annoy Miss McVinnis. You know Paula; she'll come out of this whole thing okay."

Susie and Laura chatted for a minute or two more. "Well, you'll be pleased to know that I'm going to the hospital to put in some hours this morning. I'll probably see you there."

Laura looked at the clock. "I can't believe I slept so late. That's just where I'm heading. See you." She replaced the receiver, ate a quick breakfast, and headed for the hospital.

As she checked in, Laura had to admit that she hadn't come all that way just so she could help the patients. Her motives were also a little selfish. "JoAnn, does anyone need anything delivered to X ray?" she asked the volunteer coordinator. Laura didn't know if Brad would even be there, but she did know that she had to try to see him.

"As a matter of fact, I do have a few things that should go downstairs," JoAnn replied.

Laura took the stack of brown envelopes from the third-floor nurses' station, crossed her fingers, and set out for the X ray lab.

Her heart began to pound when she saw Brad, even though she could only see the back of his head. He was looking at a screen with an X ray taped over it, and he didn't see her come in. She shuffled some of the papers and waited for him to turn around.

When he did, he said, "Oh, hi." He looked very guarded. "You can just leave those over there." Brad turned back toward the X ray. He certainly wasn't going to make this easy. But then again, she thought, she hadn't exactly made things very easy for him in the last month or so.

Even though she knew what she had to do, it took all of Laura's courage just to say, "Uh, Brad? Do you have a minute?"

"Sure," he said as he turned to face her. There was an uncomfortable silence. Suddenly, none of the things she'd planned to say seemed right. The silence grew. Laura tried to smile, but her nervousness wouldn't let her. "Uh, Brad, I just wanted to say I'm sorry—"

He cut her off. "There's no need to apologize."

Laura's eyes were full of life and pain—and warmth. "I, uh, I also wanted to let you know that I'm not going to live in the past anymore."

"Oh?" There was a spark of interest in Brad's voice, but he still sounded guarded.

Laura sighed. "Yeah. You see, the past was very special, and it's a memory I'll always have. But it was causing me to miss out on some pretty special people I know now."

"Anyone I know?" Brad had put down the X ray and came closer to her.

Laura nodded. "I think so," she half whispered.

Brad's strong arms went around her, and his lips tenderly met hers in a kiss. His arms still around her, he drew away enough to look her in the eye and ask, "You still think so?"

The part of her that always felt disloyal to Michael when she let Brad hold her disappeared. "I really do," she said.

Here's a glimpse of what's in store for you in DANGEROUS SECRETS, the fourth book in the "Sorority Girls" series for GIRLS ONLY.

Liz Moore pulled her new wool jacket around herself more tightly and hunched her shoulders against the chilly wind. The later-afternoon sunlight was beginning to fade into dusk as she walked slowly and dejectedly down Livingston Drive toward Susie Madden's house. Usually when Liz was on her way to a Pearl meeting at Susie's house, she was so full of excitement and anticipation that she almost bounced. But not today. Today's sorority meeting was not going to be an easy one, and she had to admit that she just didn't know how to handle the situation. She'd been awake all night thinking about it, and she still hadn't been able to figure out a way to solve her problem.

Liz had been a member of Pearl for nearly three years now, and sometimes it still seemed too good to be true. She almost felt like she was part of one of the fairy tales she used to make up when she was a little girl to chase away her fears of not having any friends. Sometimes she had to pinch herself to convince herself that she wasn't living in a dream.

Glumly, Liz scuffed through an ankle-deep pile of dead leaves on the sidewalk. Of course, being a Pearl wasn't always like living in a fairy tale. Sometimes—more often than she wished, really—she didn't feel that she was truly part of the group. Sometimes it almost seemed as if she'd gotten in by mistake—as if she'd lied or cheated to get that coveted invitation to pledge. It was a very uncomfortable feeling.

Liz hugged her new jacket tighter around her. Because her parents couldn't afford to give her lots of money for pretty clothes, Liz really appreciated her grandmother's surprise check. It had come at just the right time and she was finally able to buy the soft wool jacket she had been admiring at Maxi's for several weeks. Even though it had been marked down by almost half, Liz never would have been able to buy the coat without the gift from her grandmother. She sighed. The whole situation was typical. The other Pearls wouldn't have had to worry about how much the jacket cost. They would just have charged it.

Liz had discovered that for most of the Pearls, money didn't seem to matter very much. They took it for granted. But for her, not having as much as her friends always made her feel that she didn't quite belong. Maybe that was why she always felt she had to try so hard to earn everyone's respect and trust—not just in Pearl but on the Taft field hockey and tennis teams as well. And maybe that was why being elected treasurer of Pearl the previous year had meant so much to her. It meant that her friends really trusted her—at last. They trusted her enough to want her to be responsible for their money.

At the thought of money, Liz felt a cold shiver run down her back, in spite of the fact that her jacket was buttoned all the way up to her chin and she had her mittens on. Money was her biggest problem at the moment—not *her* money but the Pearls' money. And Liz had absolutely no idea what to do. The awful, bone-chilling truth was that on Sunday night, she had discovered that there was over a hundred dollars missing from the Pearls' cash box. And since she was the treasurer, she was responsible. She should have been able to account for the money, but she couldn't. She didn't have any idea what could have happened to it. It had just been gone on Sunday night when she'd counted the receipts from the Pearls' weekend car wash. And to make matters even worse, she hadn't had time to go through the account ledger to see if she'd made a mistake before the car wash. And now, at the meeting, she was supposed to give the monthly treasurer's report and tell everybody just how much money they had. In less than an hour, she was going to have to stand up in front of her sister Pearls and confess her carelessness. An icy chill ran down her back, and she shivered again. The thought of having to face the other Pearls made her feel sick to her stomach.